When Margaret left the Building

A novel by: Carys Smith

Dedicated to my daughter – this is your story too

Proof Read by: Eileen Harries
Editors: Marilyn Jenkins
             Erica Harwood
Specialist Advice: Grace Smith
Publisher: Artbully, UK>

"Fallen, fallen is Babylon the great!" Revelation 18 vs 2

Prologue:

In the year 1981 Margaret Lyse had what she would later describe as: "a flat-out Epiphany."

"It was like...you know..." she would pause, her eyes turning inward and distant in an effort to remember exactly what it had felt like, " like when your life's jigsaw suddenly slips off the edge of the table and then refuses to be put back together. All the colours and shapes have shifted and nothing fits like it used to."

She could never quite decide if the indelible sea change of heart and mind towards her faith sweeping through her within just one heartbeat was also linked to the change from Margaret to Lyse. Did that reversal of name take place at the same moment, later in the week or later still in another month entirely?

"Well, who knows?" she would say, "that was then and this is now," adding the final unarguable addendum, "what does it matter anyway? I have my truth and my truth has set
me free."

Chapter One:
Armageddon
Margaret and Eamon
1981

Margaret Lyse and Eamon Michael Hennesy sat at the back so as not to disturb the rest of the congregation. It was a long time to expect a three year old to have to sit still and today it was Margaret who suppressed a sudden urge to kick out at the back of the chair in front. Above the speaker's head an inviting blue was just visible through the skylight. She made another effort to let the commentary wash over her and joined the others flicking through their bibles to find the relevant scripture:

> **"But of that day and hour no one knows, not even the angels of heaven, but my Father only"**

For the briefest of moments Margaret was consoled by the familiar routine of finding a scripture and then considering the truth that would set mankind free. For a moment longer she remained safely ensconced in her carefully pieced together life, doggedly refusing to recognise that the shine of her religion which had once waxed so brightly had now waned; that it's golden flame of hope was about to be abruptly snuffed out.

"And so, brothers and sisters we should not give in to doubts and disappointment because the end is not yet. We should not feel that we *were* misled if as individuals *we* chose to look towards a day and hour such as 1975."

Elder Armstrong paused, his look stern and steady and intent as it dwelt on those already shuffling uncomfortably in their seats, "The words of Jesus are clear, we know not the day and hour. Those anointed amongst us *have* faithfully given us Jehovah's word through The Watchtower and are *not* those who have misled or disappointed but *we* ourselves who have gone beyond what is written."

Although Margaret and some others in the congregation, felt their eyes widen and their jaw drop imperceptibly at this outright lie for a few more blessed minutes she managed to wrestle her life into remaining the right side up. Her eyes drifted again to the skylight and then to the clock: two minutes to twelve...two minutes to Armageddon.

***

That morning as she had struggled to dress Saorise still slack with sleep, take quick bites of a banana and butter Eamon's toast she ventured a tentative suggestion.

"Why don't I keep Saorise home this morning?

Margaret had waited and then looked hopefully across at her husband who was busy scratching blue pen lines in a copy of The Watchtower and abstractedly chewing through his burnt breakfast.

"She grizzled half the night with those back teeth and I think she's developing a chesty cough."

Reluctantly Eamon lifted his eyes from the page to examine his daughter, her over bright cheeks and running nose. Should the two of them stay home again? One or other of the elders were bound to ask why. Would they decide that another absence of his wife and child was significant? Whenever he looked at his wife as he did now, he always felt a warm glow of possessive protective love. He was justly proud of her fine boned good looks and blond flyaway hair; the natural no nonsense way she had taken to the task of motherhood but lately this was tempered by a new baffled sense of unease.

He did admire her intelligent enquiring mind. Of course he did, but why had she begun to share her more controversial views outside the privacy of their own home? Why hurl so many quick-fire patently unanswerable questions at Brother Roland during the Tuesday book study? Were they honest queries or had she taken a secret perverse pleasure every time Roland had blustered and fumbled his way to yet another inconclusive answer?

He hesitated as he so often did, torn between acquiescing to his wife's common sense or the demands and expectations of those whom Jehovah had placed above them as earthly shepherds.

"Are you sure she's that poorly," he said busily folding his magazine, refusing to meet her eyes, "was she really crying half the night? I don't remember that."

Margret had begun to turn away to fetch the pushchair when she surprised them both with an irritated snap.

"How would you know Eamon?" her voice shook with a frustrated tiredness, "You just keep on snoring and I just keep on getting up."

"I think you should come," he said finally, guiltily opting to pacify the elders rather than his wife. "She might drop off to sleep."

And so Margaret complied as a godly wife should and was now sat at the back of the Kingdom Hall of Jehovah's Witnesses at one minute to Armageddon.

***

The hands of the clock clicked together. Margaret, without forethought or fear for the future, stood abruptly, dumping her well thumbed bible onto the floor, their sleeping child into Eamon's lap. Pushing through feet and knees toward the swing doors she made her unplanned dash for freedom.

"This is a load of lying bullshit," she heard herself mutter none too quietly, causing heads to turn and the speaker to falter. "Whatever god is... it's not this. I'm off!"

Eamon froze. His heart lurched and his stomach sank but somehow he forced himself to turn to one scripture after another as if nothing seismic had just happened to his wife, his life or his marriage. As Margaret, like Elvis, left the building already forming a vague plan to change her name to Lyse and find freedom he rocked his daughter in his arms and cleaved instead to the false scholarship of the chosen few.

Eamon Michael Hennesy kept his name the way it was and remained sitting upright at the back of the neat and functional Kingdom Hall whilst his wife Margaret, not quite Lyse, almost ran the few hundred yards to where an old sandstone wall was bathed in light. She leant into the healing heat of the whitewashed stone and with a deep, deep sigh of relief turned her face up to the sun.

***

As the bus pulled away Eamon was still glancing hopefully behind him. He had almost convinced himself that Margaret would suddenly materialise from the upstairs seating or would hop on at the last minute, shopping bag in hand. He waited until the final moment before he threaded his way down the crowded isle to the back seats with a fixed smile on his lips and a bewildered sense of abandonment inside. He jogged Saorise on his knee, listening to her chatter and trying not to notice the wet discomfort of his trouser thighs, counting the minutes to his escape.

By the time they reached their stop his misplaced trust in his wife had painted another rosy picture in his mind's eye: the kettle on the hob, the table laid and the pleasant odour of Sunday roast in the oven. He hurried the few remaining steps to their house bouncing and jostling the worn wheels of the pushchair, making a game of his rush, joining in with Saorise's high peeling laughter as they bumped down one curb and hurtled up the next.

He more than half expected to find the front door open in a ready welcome and his wife coming from the kitchen to greet them. The stark reality of the bare kitchen table, the scribbled note propped against the cruet set and the quiet cold kettle on the hob rocked him back on his heels as did the realisation that the only smell was the faint waft from the overnight nappy bin.

Instinct and a dim sense of dread prompted Eamon to delay picking up the note. It took a while to change Saorise and his wet trousers. Then there was the kettle to fill and a match to find to put to the gas. Eventually and with a slow hand he picked up the note and read it twice over, his mouth forming each word as if the few scant lines were clues. Why would she leave the Kingdom Hall that way? Was it really possible that she had left Saorise with him for a whole afternoon and without his Sunday dinner? Why would she want to join a swimming class with a lot of worldly people?

> **Gone to sign up for a Learn to swim class. Cold meat and salad in the fridge.**
> **Saorise's dinner in Tupperware box. Back at 4 – maybe.**

***

The queue at the newly built pool had spilled outside and an unexpected cold draught whipped at the back of Margaret's, or perhaps by now, Lyse's neck, as she stood in line with an ancient swimsuit rolled into a ragged towel and reread the crumpled food stained leaflet responsible for Eamon's lack of a Sunday dinner and Saorise's unwashed nappies.

> **Discover what swim magic means!**
> **First lesson free – yes! Free and flee if it's not for you!**
> **Join us! Feel the fear and dive in anyway!**

Her spirits lifted again as they had on first picking up the folded note from the mat along with the post. Perhaps it was the cool blue on white script, the line drawing of the red suited woman swimming swift and straight and svelte, or just the idea of opening the door a crack into another world: something forbidden? As she slowly edged forward her mouth was dry. Was it her childhood aversion of water or the fear of diving into the unknown? As the line moved forward Lyse gave up on self scrutiny, took a deep breath, inhaled the not unpleasing scent of chlorine and boldly wrote down the name Lyse Connor under ***Beginners***.

Chapter Two:
Dissent
Margaret and Eamon

Lyse Margaret missed the following two meetings. For the first she invented an excuse but by the time it was Sunday morning again she shook her head and shrugged.

"Eamon love, I really don't want to go there anymore. You know why."

Tears pricked at the back of his eyes, the small knot of anxiety he had carried with him all week turning into a rock solid boulder. He looked up from the table, his eyes shining wetly, his normally pale complexion colouring, a new formed crease between his eyebrows.

"Won't you talk to someone? Sister June maybe. You've always got on with her."

"No thanks. I've made up my own mind. We talked about it often enough. I'm going down the pool to practise my float work." As Eamon opened his mouth to protest she interrupted quickly, "Don't worry I'll have the dinner on when you get back. I can bring Saorise with me. There's a toddlers class on at the same time.

The silence between them lengthened.

"I can't allow Saorise to have swimming lessons instead of coming to meetings. Do you
 seriously think that it's right for her to mix with worldly children instead?"

"We're talking about two and three year olds Eamon. Surely they can't influence her
 either way?"

Eamon detected that new faint mockery in her tone and was saddened. Her sentence couched as a question was laced thick with irony. Why could she never resist that final provoking last word these days? Where *was* his Margaret?

He watched in silence as she turned away and plucked a new turquoise swimsuit from the drying rack. As she picked out a large blue towel emblazoned with fish, sea turtles and crabs he felt the distance between them grow. His heart dropped as she carefully placed them in a new wet bag before adding a pair of vivid blue eyed goggles. He wanted to ask her where the money had come from. He wanted to protest that she had broken their agreement not to buy things without discussing them first.

"Mum sent me twenty pounds to buy these," she said as if reading his mind. "Just look at
this little suit for Saorise. Isn't it sweet?"

He stared at the small scrap of colour and saw not its sweetness but the hand of Satan dealing a further blow to their quiet life together. He contemplated this unexpected interference from his mother in law. She had always kept a tight lipped silence about their beliefs: until now.

Driven by a desperate need to reach the security of his spiritual home he left without a goodbye and without his daughter. Too agitated to wait for the bus he strode through the new housing estate on pavements that had once been the fields of White's farm. He missed walking through the newly turned earth where he could watch the rooks and crows fight over their morning meal. He missed the evenings when the lone piper practised his melancholy marches on a foggy night from the shelter of the old Scout hut. With an effort he turned his mind away from the hurt inside his own home and the loss of yet more countryside. He reminded himself of how this estate, made up of young families, had blessed their flock. One small congregation of a few dozen had borne fruit and was now split into two.

It was a long walk but the exercise calmed his heart and eased his mind. Here he would find spiritual help and guidance. Once seated though, with an empty chair each side, a piercing awareness of his single status hit him full force. In the space of one short week how could he be sitting here wifeless, childless?

His focus refused to settle on the lesson, his tongue stumbled over favourite Kingdom songs and his own fervent prayers drowned those offered from the lectern. At last the hour break arrived and Eamon was up and out of his seat his eyes raking the crowd for Brother Leo. His six foot lanky frame and balding head was missing as was his wife, June. He glanced over at the cluster of the other elders deep in conversation just inside the doorway of a small room.

Eamon always felt uneasy when the door to that room was open and elders were in there. Apart from Leo the elders had an unflinchingly hard line approach to any spiritual opinion not originating from The Watchtower.

When the buzz in the room began to die away Eamon quickened his step to regain his seat in time. A strong hand grasped his elbow and pulled him to a sudden stop. Startled, with the beginnings of an apology forming on his lips, he realised that the hand belonged to Brother Armstrong.

"Hold on Eamon," Armstrong said nodding towards the room, "After this half we need
you to meet with us."

"Why?" said Eamon before he could stop himself. A pulse began a tick in his cheek. He flushed then paled. "I've to get back for my dinner," he added weakly, hating himself for sounding like a naughty school boy.

"Just for a few minutes Eamon," the elder persisted giving his elbow a squeeze.

Eamon's soft brown eyes widened and flinched as they met the flinty grey of Ted Armstrong's. Finally, he nodded and politely tried to release his elbow by turning to his seat and reaching for the comfort of his bible.

"Oh and bring that with you." Armstrong said as he finally relaxed his grip.

Throughout the remaining hour Eamon frantically searched his mind: he had not added or listened to any of the rumour that was rife, nor had he defended those who had fallen by the wayside. He had steadfastly obeyed the injunction to shun all whose conduct had been declared "unbecoming to a Christian" including his own brother Ian. What could he have done? Was it Margaret?

Finally something said from the platform penetrated. He leant forward thinking he must have misheard the names.

"We are saddened to announce that our former Brother and Sister Leo and June
Johnson are now disassociated from Jehovah's Witnesses. Brothers and sisters, Jehovah
is watching us to see whether we will abide by his command in Psalms 62 and 1 Corinthians 5 to shun *anyone* who has chosen to step outside his Love."

Chapter Three:
Deliverance
Lyse Margaret

Lyse Margaret lingered at the edge of the changing room as Saorise and another "Water Baby" Niamh began an intense and garbled conversation. Lyse was pleased to be forgotten, proud of her daughter's confidence and relieved. Eamon may have misgivings but here was solid evidence. Worldly three year olds were not to be feared after all.

Eager to join her class she hurried into her swimsuit. The enticing aroma of chlorine and the echo of water splash beckoned. A flyblown oblong piece of mirror screwed haphazardly to the plasterboard halted her rush momentarily. The colour and the tight fit transformed her just as Mum had predicted. An image she barely recognised smiled shyly back quickly replaced by a frown. A memory of Eamon's panic as she had folded her things into the bag begged the question: was this the look of a "godly wife"?

Lyse grabbed her goggles and shrugged marching poolside, a grown duplicate of Saorise. There was only one pressing question right now: who can show me how to stop these things leaking?

"I love your costume." A twenty something girl said as they returned to the changing room her crop of black hair shining with water drops. "What's that colour?"

Faced with a friendly question from someone "in the world" Lyse could only manage an abrupt "turquoise," before escaping to the safety of her locker.

"Turquoise? Exotic that sounds better than bluey green so. My name's Joanie, you're
Lyse aren't you?" the younger woman persisted, boldly stepping from her costume, dropping it to the floor with a practised hand.

"Yes, that's me."

Lyse bolted into one of the few private cubicles, socks and underwear falling into a puddle as she fled marvelling at the unabashed way the girl could stand stark naked calmly discussing colours.

"My sister Niamh is in the baby group with your Saorise," Joanie called after her, pushing the damp clothing under the door. "I'm nearly dressed already. I'll go get them, shall I?"

Lyse, her skirt zip sticking, her blouse buttons slipping, gave up the struggle to stay aloof.

"Thanks, I'll be a while yet."

***

Would you like a cup of tea?" Joanie asked as they stopped outside the Maddens house.

Niamh was pulling at Saorise's arm promising toys, a tea set, a dolls house, squash, chocolate.

"We must get home," Lyse said. Those two were obviously still delighted with each other.

"Alright so," said Joanie catching hold of her hand, "but won't you come up to Dunne's this
 Tuesday? They have a grand sale on. You can get yourself a comfy trackie like mine."

Lyse prepared herself to refuse: all that small talk as they had rattled the pushchair up the rocky old lane! The thought of a tracksuit was tempting though, royal blue perhaps sporting that same handsome puma motif of Joanie's?

"Saorise does need new shoes so …" Lyse hesitated a moment longer. She studied the smooth open face of Joanie, the mischievous spark in her eyes, the wide white smile. She was just a young exuberant teen. Like the infants earlier, what harm could it do?

Chapter Four:
Truth
Lyse Margaret

She cut through the estate, bumping up and down the newly laid pavements whenever she dared, flew along the rocky lane, her hair whipping back in the wind, feet off the pedals, all thoughts of bald tires and worn brake-pads an irrelevance. Shops, library, pool and tennis courts were now just a quick whiz through those awkward fields that had given way to progress.

Lyse could see Joanie already practising her serve and called a hello. She careened the final corners and was through the gate before her friend had time to wave.

"Well now," said Joanie, "that's a handsome old divil you've got there."

She slid from the saddle and pushed the bike against the fence. She pulled her racket and a tube of balls from the tattered saddlebag, her grin wide with determination.

"I've been practising with the swing ball," she warned, "Oh my! You do look smart."

"Mammy made it up for me." Joanie twirled, the short skirt lifted revealing a matching pair of frilly pants. "She'll make one for you too, if you like."

"I'd love that, but Eamon..."

"Sure, any red-blooded husband would love to see a nice bit of leg." Joanie raised an eyebrow and produced a convincing leer.

"Not mine." Lyse said, " and those elders would have a conniption fit."

Joanie stopped her ball mid bounce and studied Lyse, whose face had grown sad and serious.

"Have you got a lot of old ones living with youes?"

"Not exactly," Lyse hurried to the service line, "I'll explain later, we're only booked for
an hour.

***

"Let's have a rest," Joanie said, "that hill will kill us if we don't get a drink" she flung herself onto the grass verge and gave Lyse a searching look. "You were going to tell me about the old ones."

Lyse took a deep gulp of the lemon drink and wiped her lips with the back of her hand. She fiddled with the lid. She looked across at the remaining field now tall with corn, commented on the heat of the day, the sounds of children's voices ringing in the quiet air until Joanie prodded her with a foot and said,
"Come on would you ever spill."

Lyse glanced at Joanie and then away. What would happen if she did "spill?" Would the ground open and swallow her down if she finally told herself the truth? Told Joanie, a good Catholic girl, who Lyse Connor really was?

"First off," said Lyse finally, "My proper name is Margaret Lyse Hennesy and I was one of
Jehovah's Witnesses, but I don't think I am anymore."

Words, explanations, clarifications, reasons, confusions, all tumbled from her in their hurry to be set free. Joanie chewed grass stalks in a rare silence until Lyse arrived at her final destination.

"Actually I think it's all a lot of brainwashing rubbish," she said with a heady sense of
freedom. Had the simple act of truthful speech washed her confusion clean away? "I was only 16 when I got involved and now I can't believe I've been so dense all these years."

"Well," said Joanie spitting out grass, "Shite. What a story."

"Yes, shite is the word." Lyse agreed, deciding that a profanity may as well add to her
growing list of sins.

The two resumed their walk taking turns to force the cycle up through the uneven lane and into the estate, Joanie unaccustomedly silent. Half way as they paused to catch their breath
Lyse surprised herself with a suggestion.

"Why don't we pick up Niamh and bring her to my house? You can meet my Eamon. He's
 a lovely man. You'll like him."

***

With barely a glance at her mother Saorise flew through the open door and flung herself at Niamh with a yell of delight.

"I told thems you was out with your bats and ball!" she called from the staircase. "Can
Niamh stay for dinner...and tea Mammy?"

Lyse looked back onto the street. A battleship grey Ford was parked haphazardly a few doors down. She went to the drivers' window. There was a pile of Watchtower and Awake magazines, a notebook and a familiar smart fedora hat on the driver's seat. The deep bass of Elder Armstrong, the lighter tones of Flowers and the respectful pitch of the younger Berri filtered through the half open door.

"What are they doing here?" Lyse barely dropped her voice, "I wanted you to meet Joanie. I don't want to see them."

Eamon had come from the kitchen backwards and had turned awkwardly, the tea tray lurching, their best china slipping.

"I asked them not to wait but they..." Eamon caught sight of their visitor and flushed. The voices inside the best room faltered as Joanie, still in her tennis kit, skipped across the threshold.

"Howya Eamon." she said with her big white grin, hand outstretched. "Opps! You can't shake so." She leant forward and pecked his cheek instead. Her lips twitching as she glimpsed the scowling faces from the living room.

"Will you tell them or will I?" Lyse said.

Eamon stared at his wife, her friend, the door ajar, the stone faced elders, his cheeks now flaming. He handed the tray to Margaret Lyse.

"Won't you just..." he began.

"I'll do it then," she said, "Joanie can you get the girls from upstairs."

She elbowed aside the door and banged the tray onto the dresser.

"Help yourselves."

"Just a moment Sister Margaret," Ted Armstrong held out his bible face forward. "You must sit down and talk with us. Show some respect for Jehovah's appointed shepherds."

Lyse, momentarily Margaret hesitated, years of habit warring with her new self. She ignored the beseeching look from her husband standing close beside her. She studied the narrow stern face of Armstrong, the jowly set jaw of Flowers and the uncertain features of Berri.

"I'm not Sister anything and you're just men." She forced eye contact with each one in
turn adding, "not men I have to talk to." She said, her voice firm."Talk to Eamon if you like. I'm going to the park."

***

"Those Jova's are really something aren't they?" said Joanie to Lyse once the girls
were settled in the sandpit and she had joined her on the bench. "I should ditch them
and keep the husband if I was you."

Lyse had arrived in a mood high, triumphant, yet now she stared down at her shoes. An unwanted insight was leaving its icy imprint around where she imagined her heart to be.

"Yes, that was the plan" Lyse said her attempted smile fading, her complexion ashen. "I
forgot. They never let anyone just leave. They have to judge and punish and say it's the will of Jehovah."

Tears began to leak from her eyes and slip unchecked onto the grass between her feet. Why had she believed she was untouchable, different from all the others who had tried to escape unharmed. No one who dared ever managed to keep their lives, their family intact.

Chapter Five:
Love is...
Eamon

Eamon made his way up to the spare room his feet echoing in the unnatural silence. The elders had finally left. Margaret and Saorise had not yet returned. He closed the door and crossed to the window, snapped the Venetian blind shut and switched on his table lamps. He examined the sketches he had finished the day before and pushed them aside. The composition did not work. He would have to start again. Not today though. Not now. He put down the charcoal pencil and stepped away into the middle of the room looking for something that would settle him.

He began to sort through his paints; separating them into primary and secondary colours, then divided tubes of acrylic from oils, before turning to his brushes. There was a glass jar of discoloured turps where two of his best Kolinsky's still languished. He knew even before he examined them that the glue would have begun to separate from the bristles. They should have been safely in the linseed oil on the next shelf. It had been careless and not like him.

As he snatched at the brushes the jar tipped. He watched the stain eat into the carpet wondering briefly how he would ever get it out. With a sudden angry movement he swept the entire contents off the workbench. A box of crimson powder paint, the linseed oil, coloured chalks and an open bottle of blue ink spiralled down to join the party. Still not satisfied he ripped at his sketches and sent the pieces scattering into the mess turned on his heel and went down the stairs at a run.

Eamon made for the park jogging steadily only slowing once he heard his daughter's familiar musical laugh drifting up across the field. He would tell Margaret everything. He would admit his doubts. He would describe the awful way the elders had bludgeoned him with scriptures. He would share his view that the dear Lord Jesus would not wish any Kingdom Hall to have a Room of

Reproof. He would tell her about Brother Leo and Sister June, he would... his fast pace began to slow as the distant figures became clear. Margaret, his Margaret was seated on the bench with that friend, Joanie. Their heads were close, touching almost, their hands joined, their conversation obviously intense. His slow steps finally halted. His hand unconsciously went to his heart as it twisted, his head swam, his eyes blurred.

"Love is not jealous..." he muttered, now knowing what it meant to see red, "love is
not jealous" he said again, "love believes all things, hopes all things, love is not jealous.
Is *not, not* jealous..."

Eamon desperately repeated his mantra with every step retraced but knew, as his heart continued to thump painfully, that he was, he was.

***

For the second time that day Margaret Lyse said, "I want to be called Lyse."
Eamon looked up from his sketch book, the page unturned, his mouth dropping open
in surprise.

"You want me to call you Lyse?"

"Why not?" she reached across and took his hand, "It's my middle name. I've always
preferred it to Margaret."

Eamon carefully withdrew his hand. The picture of his wife and her friend still burned. He turned the page. Lyse began to clear their plates and fill the washing up bowl before coming
back to the table.

"And I don't believe any of it anymore. I truly think we've been brainwashed. Look at the evidence for yourself."

He turned another page his eyes fastened on his book, heart beginning to race once more. Those words were apostasy. Not doubts but serious dissent. What did she expect him to say? What did he want to say?

After a long silence she said "will you help me get that crate down from the loft? I've got
the ladder in from the shed."

"Why?" he snapped the book shut and finally faced his wife, "Why do you want all those
old magazines? Most of them are full of old thinking from 1925 or even earlier. Things
we don't believe anymore."

"Because I need to," she took a step forward, wiping soapy hands on her apron, "Eamon.
Love. Something is wrong with their teachings. You know that. I know you do."

"I only know that since you've started all this swimming and tennis there's something
 wrong with you. And now you don't want to be Margaret, my Margaret," his voice rose "you want to be Lyse and hang around with that young one Joanie, like you're a teenager
and not a mother and a wife!"

He pushed back his chair, the legs scraping along the oilcloth with a force that left a dirty mark.

"Look it..." he said, his anger evaporating at the sight of Lyse's stricken face. "I'll take
them down for you only...only I don't want to talk about it. Not now, anyway."

"When?" Lyse followed him into the hall and called after his retreating back. "Eamon.
Please. We have to talk about this."

Eamon disappeared into the loft space as Lyse hesitated on the bottom step. Finally there was a resounding thump and then another and another as decades of yellowing, oversized pages of The Watchtower and Awake were thrown from the hatch and began to cascade
down the stairway to arrive at her feet.

***

"That's a god awful smell you've got there," said Joanie. She wrinkled her nose and held up the magazine with her finger tips.

Lyse peered at her friend through a gap in the bundles of ancient Watchtowers stacked high on the kitchen table. "It's the chemicals and the paper and print is all," she said, "the stinking smell of evidence you might say."

"What a stinking message too. " Joanie shook her head at the lurid depiction of Jehovah's thunderbolt striking the innocents and dropped it back down.

Lyse carried on working through the faded water stained pages of an old blue covered text book, carefully recording numbers, dates and underlining relevant passages. Joanie shrugged and pulled out a bottle of Guinness from her kit bag and watched for a while, one eye on the clock, anticipating their first ever doubles tennis match to come.

"Here it is!" Lyse said finally, her voice lifting in excitement, "See, six thousand years ending
 Autumn 1975." She flicked over a few pages her finger stabbed at a crude chart, her pen etching a deep circle in red around it.

Joanie stared down at the chart and then up at Lyse, "The end of what? Excuse me for saying so but isn't it 1981, even as I speak?"

"Look here's my name: Sister Margaret L Connor 1966. I was there. I've studied this book. I was baptised at that Convention." Lyse danced a quick jig. "We all believed the end was to come in 1975. That's what we were told and now I can prove it to Eamon."

"Well then so." Joanie fished about in her bag and found another bottle, "Will we drink to that before we go?"

Lyse hesitated. Alcohol? How many sins was it now?

"Ok why not? To the stinky smell of truth and…" she wavered briefly, "and after the match and when we've picked up the girls from KidsPlay I want to find a public telephone that works."

Joanie raised an eyebrow, "No chance. Come up and use ours. Who are you wanting
to call?"

"Leo and June Johnson." Lyse said, pushing their names from her throat with something akin to dread. Was this to be her biggest sin of all? "I'm going to call them. I'm going to ask them to come round and see Eamon. That's what I'm going to do."

Lyse took a long deep slug of the dark velvet astonished by the silken taste of something so sinful. Once she had made that call there would be no turning back. It would make the accusation of dissent unarguable but if she could get Eamon to listen their little family would stay safe.

"To the stinky smell of truth!" they both intoned and raised their bottles to the heavens.

Chapter Six:
The Advancing Light
Leo and June

Leo replaced the telephone and frowned into the mirror. Was God's will that he should become the conduit of all those disaffected by the behaviour of the Governing Body? If it was then he had a Christian duty he could not shirk even though it would bring more trouble and most likely alienate them even further from their children. He took off his glasses and polished them vigorously. He opened the appointments diary and hunted for next Wednesday's date. He pencilled in a name and glanced through the open door at June who was pretending to be absorbed in her knitting. He could tell by the tense lift of her shoulders and tight set of her lips that she was hoping he would say the call had been from Simon or Martha. He sighed. Neither of their children had been in touch since that Sunday. They had taught them only too well. They would obey the Governing Body's shunning edict to the letter.

"I just want to have a look at something in the study," he called, "won't be long."

June nodded and redoubled her efforts with the pattern, slumping a little further into the sofa. Fifty years of marriage had taught her the art of waiting. Whoever or whatever it was, Leo would tell her in his own good time: or he would not. She set aside her work and contemplated their new acquisition. It had been nice to be able to buy it and not feel guilty but apart from the news and the occasional wildlife programme the television reposed quietly in its corner as a statement of freedom rather than one of entertainment.

She looked at her watch. It was only just after three. Monday at this time used to be one of her busiest days; door to door with Lynette, a bible study with the Wallace's and then a quick dash home to set the tea table for the after school pick up. She had begun to count the empty hours of each day by its losses; her children; her grandchildren; her friends; her spiritual activities; her God. Leo was right to have taken his stand. Of course he was. A man like him would have had no choice but to speak out, to insist on the truth and to oppose the wrongs the Governing Body was imposing on those that questioned their lies and faulty prophecy. But the penalty had fallen heavy on her. Leo had soon found a new outlet for his zeal, whereas she...

"Look" said Leo on his return. He brandished the same blue book Lyse had been reading earlier. Their eyes met. His were eager, his face flushed with his discovery. He was bristling with excitement. 'Life Everlasting in the Freedom of the Sons of God,' remember it?"

"Of course I do." June felt the dull ache of betrayal begin again. "It changed our lives. It gave us all false hope and made us reckless with the future of our children."

Leo sat down next to her, "I know dear," he said, "but this book and the rest of our archive can perhaps go some way to set them free."

"Who called Leo?" June said, "Was it..."

"No. Not Simon or Martha. Not yet anyway but it *was* Margaret Hennessey. She has an archive just like ours."His faint optimism grew, "she wants us to help her with Eamon and then, well, isn't it possible they might be able to reach out to Simon and Martha? The four of them practically grew up together."

June took the book from his hands and turned it over once or twice. She thought about the vast collection of evidence they had painstakingly recorded, the draft copy of Raymond Franz's book they had received only this morning. She thought about the gaping wound where her children and grandchildren should be and nodded with the same slow sense of returning hope as her husband.

"Why not ask her to come here first?" she said."Perhaps I could compare her findings with ours before you talk to her and before we even think of approaching Eamon?"

"That's exactly what I thought."Leo was relieved."I've put down Wednesday morning for you. Do you mind?"

"No not a bit." June struggled up pushing her half finished jumper aside, "I'll make us a quick tea and then we can go into the study and get together our best evidence."

Leo looked after his wife's small rounded figure as she hurried into the kitchen. Was she stooping a little less? Was there light after all in the darkness that leaving behind a lifetime of mistaken service had dealt them?

***

Lyse and June

Lyse rang the Johnson's bell three times in quick succession. The road was a small cul-de - sac that housed more than just one Witness family. She suppressed the urge to look behind, trying not to look furtive. This was *not* Satan's doorstep no matter what hysterical commentary was coming from the Watchtower these days. Leo and June were the same kindly couple she had known since a teenager. Still she wished the footsteps she could hear on the stairs would make their way to the door so that she could slip inside unnoticed.

For a moment Lyse could not place what was different in the room. The chintzy curtains and well-worn dark blue three piece suite had not changed. The family photographs still decked the mantelpiece and June was pouring their tea from the usual brown tea pot into a pair of matching mugs.

"Ah, that's it," she said, "now I see it. You've got a television set."

"Yes, we got one," June said, "but I can't see what the fuss is about. We don't watch it much."

Lyse took a closer look at its highly polished mahogany casing and rounded screen. At the very least it was a nice piece of furniture. Joanie's family had one just like it. Saorise loved watching theirs, especially that Sesame Street. Eamon though detested them and did not need the Governing Body to forbid it.

"But at least you could go out and buy one," she said, "*and* decide not to watch it for yourself!"

"There is a certain kind of freedom in being able to decide I suppose," conceded June. Her eyes left the television and lingered on her family portraits before their faded blue returned to Lyse, giving her a long searching look.

Lyse became acutely aware of the quiet ticking clock, the faint sounds of a child crying through the wall and of the way her own anxieties must be written on her face.

"Is it worth it?" she said at last "Just to be proved right about a mistaken date?"

June set down her mug and began her slow efforts to rise, "If it was only 1975 then
I would have counted our losses as too great but..." she hesitated and gave the younger woman another lengthy, considering look, "but if you are prepared to find out how far
they have failed all of us then we should go on into the study."

***

Lyse decided to walk rather than bus home from Tallaght grateful that Joanie was with the girls and that Eamon was going to be late. She needed to think and her head was foggy, full of disconcerting facts and worrying conclusions that could not be explained away. She shifted the heavy carrier bag from one hand to the other. It held a huge Xeroxed copy of the draft book the Johnson's friend, Raymond Franz was in the process of having published.

She and June had discussed a number of chapters all of which appeared to present meticulous incontrovertible proof that their lives had not been governed by a loving God, but by an organisation led by just a few prominent men whom insisted on harsh punishments wanting to silence anyone who dared question their interpretations regardless of scriptural evidence to the contrary.

Lyse rested on a bench and tried without success to tune into the birdsong from the trees behind. How was she going to tell Eamon where she had been? How was she going to persuade her sincere devout husband that their life was built on nothing but dogmatism and false prophecy? He had given up so much: his advertising career, his acting and of course, his brother Ian.

For the rest of the walk she continually returned to the sad sense of loss that seemed to emanate from June whenever she had glanced at the mantelpiece. Somehow, although the afternoon was sultry and warm she felt a chill wind at the back of her neck where there was none. Whatever happened she must somehow, someway, keep her little family together.

Chapter Seven:
Truth or Tyranny
Lyse and Eamon

The six o clock Angelus reverberated throughout the estate. Eamon shrugged off his jacket and shut the door on St Gilbert's. He had hoped for a house further away where the sound would be fainter. The tolling bells were a sad reminder of his bleak Catholic boyhood and miserable schooling with the Christian Brothers.

The unexpected aroma of roasted chicken and potatoes lifted his spirits as he crossed to the kitchen. He hesitated in the doorway as he took in the vase of garden cornflowers, the candle and glint of wine glasses. He counted two placemats, two sets of cutlery, two glasses, one half bottle of white wine and was relieved. His in-laws rarely visited but these days he was never sure what Margaret Lyse would think up next.

"Surprise!" said his wife with a wide grin as she stirred something in a pot. Eamon's eyes widened in pleasure at the sight of his wife in his favourite sky blue cotton dress rather than the mix and match sportswear she seemed to prefer these days.

"Surprise indeed!" he said and sat down returning her smile, pouring them both a drink, "Where's our Saorise? She's never in bed is she?"

"No. She's spending the night with Niamh." Lyse said leaving the stove and taking the glass he offered, "You should have seen her excitement when we packed up her night things in that little cardboard case you made her."

Eamon looked at his radiant wife who had left her blond hair untied, inhaled the fruity scent of his wine, anticipated his dinner and the rare opportunity of the two of them spending some time alone. He decided not to raise the issue of the night away with all those worldly Maddens.

***

"I'll wash the dishes tomorrow," said Lyse as Eamon began to fill the sink, "You sit down again and I'll make us a cup of tea to finish."

"Will we have an early night then?" said Eamon reaching for her hand. "I don't mind about the tea." He leaned in and kissed her cheek. Lyse clung to his hand momentarily and then seemed to shake herself before stepping away.

"That will be nice love. And we will," she said, "but can we sit down and have a bit of a
talk first do you think?"

"Can't it wait until tomorrow?" Eamon pressed but Lyse had already gone over to the cupboard and was taking out a heavy cardboard box and a large plastic bag full of papers. He recognised the unpleasant musty smell and the yellowish pages as those he had taken from the loft and sat down heavily, folding his arms. He considered her pretty dress and loose hair with fresh sullen eyes. A tide of disappointment and irritation swept over him as he thought too about the carefully cooked meal, the nicely laid table and the rare addition of wine.

"Eamon," faltered Lyse. His normally pleasant features were creased, his mouth thin. He had begun to rock on the two back legs of his chair. Finally she continued with a rush, "I went to see Leo and June on Wednesday and I really need to talk to you about what ..."

Eamon stared across the table at his wife and let the chair down with a thump.

"Margaret!" he went to the windows and pulled them shut, "Don't you realise how dangerous that was?"

"No one saw me Eamon." Lyse watched him pace the length of their small galley kitchen. "No one saw me," she repeated.

"But now *I* know," he said, his voice rising in panic, "and you've got things in that bag that I can see must be from them."

"Them are our friends Eamon!"

"They *were* our friends." His voice stuttered and his hands shook as he picked up the box, "and now you've brought their apostasy into our house!"

Lyse slid the carrier bag out of his reach and into her lap, "This is not apostasy. It's truth!"

Eamon's eyes met hers and then darted away as if he could not bear to look at this stranger posing as his wife. "I've got to tell the elders," he said his voice low, "or they'll disfellowship me as well as you."

They sat in the long silence that followed until the sky began to turn dusky grey and the sun had sunk low behind the garden wall. Lyse eventually gave up and left the room taking everything with her save a small red notebook which she placed carefully in front of him.

Eamon slumped further into his chair and kept his head down as her footsteps climbed the stairs. He resisted the desperate longing to follow; hold her close and reassure her that he would keep their secret; to somehow erase the growing distance between them. He fingered the corners of the notebook. With the same furious anger of the art room, he began to rip and tear into it before hurling the screwed up remains into the sink. He waited until the blue ink began to bleach into the soapy water and vowed to burn every last thing Lyse had taken with her: to save his marriage he would make his peace with Jehovah God and say nothing.

It was quiet in the kitchen and lonely with just the candle lit. He thought of his lovely Margaret perhaps still awake and waiting for him upstairs. Tomorrow he would persuade her to give up this insanity but tonight he would mend their marriage as best he could.

In the flickering of faint light his eye caught a glimpse of a ripped sheet beneath his feet. He kicked his foot free and lifted the half page taking it to the sink. He would drown this lie with the rest: ***blood transfusion – did I refuse because of scripture or because of threats from the organisation – a spiritual tyranny?*** It was definitely written in Margaret's unmistakable hand.

His fingers started to crumple the words and then abruptly relaxed. He studied them, noted the scriptures from Genesis, Leviticus and Acts and then a date printed in capitals: **JUNE 1 1969 P326-327** and slowly took his hand away from the water.

Eamon knew these verses by heart as every Witness did. That article he had only read once. When? A cloudy memory of a day three and a half years ago abruptly leapt back into full view: Margaret prone on the hospital bed whey faced; his trembling grip of her hand and Brother Armstrong standing behind reading scripture and offering up prayers. That brief comfort draining away outside the closed curtains as he was handed the article and directed to read it carefully: to be in no doubt of the consequences if either he or she weakened in their resolve.

He smoothed out the note folding it carefully before shoving it deep into his trouser pocket. He pulled the plug and waited for the water to drain and then carefully cleared the residue of inky pulp into the scraps bin. He refilled the sink with hot soapy suds and took his time washing and drying every dish and spoon before gutting the candle and locking the back door. They had resolutely taken their stand to "abstain from blood" and thankfully she had recovered but had it been pure faith in the word of their God or fear of judgement and punishment from earthly men who through the pages of the Watchtower were exacting a "spiritual tyranny?"

Eamon silently changed and slipped into bed wrapping a protective arm about Margaret Lyse's waist gently pressing his head against her familiar soft body. For a while he listened to her quiet breathing waiting for the sleep that was slow to come. They had very nearly lost her. He tried to picture his and Saorise's life without her and drew a deep dark blank.

***

Eamon was uneasy. The girls had left. His studio door was locked but still his conscience pricked: he had failed his all seeing all knowing God. The second chapter of A *Crisis of Conscience* sat square on his cleared desk unscathed, still whole. He switched on his side lamp and considered the heading of Chapter Two and then the quotation from Romans 9:1-3: "***I am speaking truth as a Christian, and my own conscience enlightened...***"

His initial reluctance, as with the first chapter, dissipated. He began to read with an avidity that frightened him thrusting aside each completed page, hurriedly turning to the next and then the next hardly noticing the daylight begin to fade until the chapters' end. It was only when Saorise's shrill excited cries of "Da! we be home. Da! we be home" that he thought to glance at his watch.

He smoothed the papers back into shape stealthily returning them to the cupboard then leapt down the stairs two at a time to escape their burning truths or lies.

"It my darlings, Lyse and Saorse!" he said swinging the little girl round grinning at his wife's delighted surprise at the use of her chosen name. "Home again home again Lysidy Lyse and what's for our tea?"

"Whatever you want love." she said, "Whatever we've got anyways."

Eamon laughed and joked and smiled as he used to as if their fragile harmony was completely restored. His mind though still worried and picked and replayed the final sentence from Raymond Franz: **"this book is offered to be applied in whatever way your conscience may lead..."**

Chapter Eight:
Hypocrites and Pharisees
Lyse and Ian

Lyse waved at Eamon until he was just a small grainy speck turning the corner before going inside to finish her chores and think about his clothes. They were tidy enough for Saturday field service but that hand knitted blue and yellow stripy woollen cap was the one he only wore to visit his Mam.

How many times had he worn that cap lately? Was he really going on field service or was his briefcase strapped to the crossbar just to look as if he was? How many meetings might he have missed? How many more pages of that book was he going to read in secret? Lyse could still feel these questions on the tip of her tongue. The memory of his strained pale face and the way his eyes had slid away from hers this morning hurt. Had her face held such a look when leaving June last week?

Lyse went into the back yard her spirits lifting at the sight of Eamon's surprise gift. The fresh layer of purple paint gleamed and the lamps sparkled. The saddle was new and was set at the correct height; the basket up front was big enough to carry all her shopping plus her swim kit. There was a handy bell just by the front brake. It was a lovely thoughtful gift and she knew without being told; given to reaffirm and reassure her of his love.

She set off hopeful, the well oiled chain silently efficient, tyres plump with air and on the lookout to try the bell. The hectic free fall downhill blew aside all thoughts save the idea of getting a sturdy lock to protect her beautiful present. She made a shaky left hand signal and swung up to Madden's Hardware hoping to find Joanie.

When a greeting of "Margaret what about youes?" met her as she wheeled her bike inside she was slow to react to the name and to the familiar male voice of her brother- in -law. For a moment they regarded each other with a strange mix of shy wariness.

"How'ya Ian," Lyse said propping her bike against the open door. "I've come to buy a lock. Want to give me some advice?" Lyse saw his shoulders sag a little in relief and was stung.

"Then maybe we can go to Doyles for a drink?" he suggested, voice low and tentative.

Ian waited staring down at his shoes his hands in his pockets. Lyse pretended not to see the glint of a tear in the corner of his eye. He was just as prone to tears as his older brother. She picked out a long chain attached to a huge padlock and weighed it in both hands.

"Now, what do you think of this beastie?" she said, adding "and I don't care who sees us," she gave him an arch grin. "I'm Lyse now not Sister Margaret. I can think for myself."

***

"You and your brother are so like, you know." Lyse squeezed his hand as they waited to cross the busy road. "He'll never let me cross without taking my arm either." Quick to see the downturn of his lips at the mention of his elder brother she gave his hand another squeeze and hurried him over and into the lounge bar.

"Will our Eamon speak to me now do you think?" Ian said picking at the edge of a beer mat.

"Well I'm talking to you aren't I?" she said, gently taking the beer mat from his fingers.

"But *will* our Eamon speak to me now?" Ian asked again. "Tell him Declan's not a bad man. He just asked questions about 1975 is all and I really need the work. There's Maeve and the baby won't be long in coming."

"None of this makes sense."Lyse was careful not to promise. "All you've done is work to feed your family."

Lyse looked across at Ian. He was hardly a man yet what with his wispy beginnings of a moustache and the way he still flushed when forced to speak up for himself. How could they have let this happen? How was it possible that she had ever thought it right to shun anyone for so little reason? Did her lovely and loving husband still believe that to abandon his own brother was the will of a just and loving God?

"They come in here of a Saturday you know," he said shifting his glance to the windows and then to the door, "for their coffee after field service. If I'm doing a shift they wait for someone else to serve them."

Lyse had forgotten that Saturday ritual. It already seemed a world away: a world she had easily airbrushed aside replacing it with less demanding pursuits and far less judgemental friends. Yet Ian was made of a different metal. He was like his brother, a soft and gentle man.

"I'll talk to him tonight Ian," she said, "I will."

"Thanks."Ian said, "Do you think you can get him to see me? "

Lyse wrinkled her nose as Ian took out a tobacco tin from his overalls pocket and started to roll a thin cigarette.

"Eamon won't be delighted to see you smoking those things," she said edging her chair away. "When did you start back on them?"

"I don't know exactly," he said putting the blue flame to paper, "but what have I got to lose now anyways? I might as well be hung for a sheep as a …" Ian trailed off and threw a shy smile at his sister- in-law.

Lyse grinned back a gurgle of laughter rising in her throat, "that's a good pun Ian lad…a sheep as a… a goat?"
"Baa.Baa." said Ian taking a long drag, "Baa. Baa. Baa." he repeated blowing smoke rings at her.

"Baa. Baa." Lyse wafted aside the silver grey spirals. "Baa. Baa. Baa."

Ian smirked and sent another across the table squawking exactly like the rooster his Daideo had kept in the yard to service the hens.

"Stop that Ian Hennessey." Lyse hissed helpless with laughter as heads turned, adding a snort a low moo and a series of convincing clucks.

As silly as teenagers they snickered into their hands: they cackled and chirped and baa'd, their shoulders heaving in silent pained mirth, hot tears leaking, falling unchecked onto the beer-sticky table top.

***

Lyse and Ian walked back to Madden's Hardware light headed and shriven. Pulling on her jacket against the drizzle the cold stares from a huddle of smart men and women with familiar telltale bags and briefcases drew her eye. Lyse stood tall and returned their stare waiting until they studiously turned their heads.

"Now you're for it," said Ian anxiety creeping back into his face, "I'm sorry."

"Don't you dare apologise." Lyse said. "Hypocrites, Pharisees!" she called, rage giving her voice piercing clarity. "Baa. Baa. Baa!"

Chapter Nine:
Prayers
Eamon and Mam

Eamon was not preaching with his brothers and sisters. He was taking the costal path to Drogheda. With heavy legs he struggled uphill against the windy drizzle in his inadequate T shirt. He wished he had suggested a family day out on the bus and train. Saorise would have loved that. Mam would ask why she was left behind although probably not mention the absence of his English wife.

At the half way mark he slid off his bike and almost fell onto a bench. He sat with his head gratefully thrown back to catch the salt spray and the bracing sea air. There was nothing behind except the dunes full of beach grass and before him the vast choppy green sea. He followed the flight of a lone gull, remembered the ebb and flow of human misery from fragments of Arnold's poem and struggled to find the familiar comfort of prayer. The words continually died on his lips. Doubt swallowed all thoughts leaving only questions: where was truth if not within his religion? Who was God if not Jehovah? Is this what Lyse meant when she had walked away with the words "Whatever God is...?"

***

Eamon mended the drawer and unblocked the sink whilst Mam read out the Obituaries and described in detail funerals she had attended during the past weeks. Eamon said little feeling as if he had taken the place of his father who had always listened cowed and respectful whilst she talked of the dead, the Masses made and the quality of the Wakes.

"I pray to St Jude every single day for you and your brother." Mam said putting the paper to one side.

Eamon observed her slow gait as she crossed the room. Her hand shook as she struck a match to light another votive candle. White had completely replaced the dark hair. The once ramrod back was a pronounced stoop. She was faded and shrunken. He went back to working on the drawer and tried to blot out the fierce judgements of her prayers.

"Will we have a cup of tea together before I go Mam?" Eamon said.

"Fill the kettle then." She said and genuflected before the cheap print of the Patron for Hopeless Causes.

He switched on the kitchen light hoping that it might dispel the gloom that always settled throughout the house every afternoon. The dim orange glow made little difference. It was not just the old fashioned under sized windows or the thick net curtains. The entire house always seemed to breath out a grim brand of Catholic guilt; an unchanging pervasive sense of unworthiness that wrapped itself around him as soon as he stepped through the door.

He waited for the kettle to boil and pictured the emaciated figure of his Da trapped in the armchair in that dispiriting house always in half light. His eyes watered. The poor man had hardly been able to breath for the cough that devoured him. Eamon wanted to change the subject and lift his growing despair with chatter about Saorise or his work but instead drank his tea quickly and left early.

***

The jumper Mam gave him was the last she had knitted for his father. It was warm but tighter across the chest and under the arms than he had expected. He stopped to take it off wrapping it carefully into the saddlebag. Why had that fun loving and gentle man picked such a stern and unbending woman to be his wife? He searched his heart for love but could only find pity and a certain respect. His Margaret Lyse was a strong woman too but along with her serious side he loved her kindness and patience especially with Saorise. Da would have liked her even Lilly and Cara did and they, like their Mam, were fierce Catholics. Mam had never taken to her. She had never a good word to say about her. She had asked whether it was true that his wife was mixing with the Maddens and running around with a lot of girls playing games."

"It's not natural Eamon." She had told him her lips thin with satisfaction, "a married woman, with a child, running all over the place with young ones."

Eamon had said nothing. He knew he should have defended Lyse but for once was in silent agreement with his mother. There *was* something unnatural about it all. What *was* she doing dressing up like a boy and playing at being a teenager?

His heart squeezed as it had when he had seen his wife's hand in Joanie's. He smothered the panic, pushing away his unworthy suspicions and the gossip he had heard about some of those girls. He sat for a long while looking out at the unfathomable seascape. He fought hard until he found the will to break his long silence and pray to his God: Jehovah.

He resumed the journey with a mind returned to its old clarity, his shaky faith completely restored. As his tyres ate away at the miles he determined to burn all those apostate writings. He would explain that their sane and sensible religion was there to keep them and Saorise safe. If he passed this test and returned to the "truth" then Jehovah would surely take away this incomprehensible Lyse and return him his true love, his Margaret.

Chapter Ten:
Torn
Lyse

It was Saorise who spotted the smoke first. Its column of pale grey-blue smoke rose above the back fence spitting blackened shards of floating paper to the wind.

"Oh nasty!" she said as they opened the gate and saw Eamon thrusting piles of paper into the fire, "nasty and smelly Da."

Lyse took Saorise's arm jumping away as twigs snapped and a rush of air collided with the paraffin soaked print.

"Eamon! If you must have a bonfire at least use some of the kindling. Here." She pulled open the coal shed took out a handful and thrust it at his feet. "That fly away paper is dangerous. Lookit! Next door still has their washing on the line."

Eamon said nothing. He bent down and picked up the sticks throwing twigs, an old painting and more pages into the flames.

Lyse stood in a moment of indecision her hand firmly in Saorise's who snuffled at the cloying sweet smell wafting her ineffectual small hand at the bright blaze. She stared at her father's turned back and the tumbling burning paper. She looked up at Lyse her bottom lip trembling.

"What's wrong with Da Mammy? Is the papers bad?"

"I'm going to make us our tea now." Lyse said squeezing her hand. "We'll go in and let Da finish his job."

Lyse watched from the window until Eamon had burned the book and every last one of the Watchtowers. She stayed at the sink until she was sure he had stamped out every flicker. She filled the wash up basin and took it out to him without a word waiting until he had emptied it onto the stinking smouldering heap.

Throughout the near silent meal Lyse ached at the way Saorise was casting anxious glances across at her father who sat with a pale and mutinous look picking at his food before pushing aside his plate. Lyse took Saorise away as soon as the meal was done and spent a long time playing with her in the bath and reading stories until she finally drifted off to sleep. She listened to the clatter of washing dishes and the run of water from the sink. She held onto the sleeping fingers through the cot bars and rubbed tears away with the back of her hand. She wished for Eamon's step on the stair and for him to come up for her, his face returned to its amiable self. She hoped until she heard the back door slam shut and the back gate open and the rattle of his bike go through.

***

Eamon

The drizzle turned heavy on his way home and the wind sharpened. He stood on the pedals and leaned over the handlebars for the final hill. He welcomed the hard work; the complete focus of the climb that briefly quieted his mind. On his arrival he saw the kitchen light was still on. Lyse was reaching up into the cupboard and turned as his wheels clicked to a halt. Their eyes met through the window and Eamon smiled faintly uneasy with his news.

"Here's a cup of tea love" Lyse said. "Take off that jacket and dry yourself by the fire."

Eamon shook the waterproof and hung it over a chair kicked off his boots and stood irresolute in the middle of the room his hands dangling helplessly by his sides. His face coloured with effort his throat closed on the words he had been commanded to say. With slow steps he went to the chair nearest the small fire Lyse had built and took the proffered mug in both hands. He stared at the reproachful glowing coals and wished he could apologise for setting the bonfire so carelessly and without warning, for frightening Saorise with his pale face, for failing to protect his wife.

In the silence that followed Eamon drew some comfort from the familiar sounds of Lyse putting the kitchen to rights, the curtains pulled, the table laid for breakfast, the snap from the lid of his sandwich box, the low glow of the corner light coming on. He cautiously sipped at his tea and shrank away from what had to come next.

"Eamon?" Lyse said finally, "Where did you go off to?"

Eamon shook his head and set the mug at his feet. He crossed to the sink and poured a glass of water throwing it down in one gulp. He refilled the glass with a shaking hand. His mouth felt dry and his tongue swollen. His lips opened and closed.

"I had to tell them," he hurried through his news. "I thought if I burned everything and then told them that...that... that they might not...might not..."

Lyse took away the glass and placed it carefully in the sink. She took his hands forcing him to look down at her. "Has nothing you've read convinced you that we need to get away from them?"

Eamon flushed. "You knew..."

"Of course I did. But what made you come home today and burn everything and none of it yours to burn?"

"It's apostate. I prayed about it. I decided. I burned it." Eamon said as his earlier conviction resurfaced. "I wanted us to go back to the way we were." His voice shook with frustration and alarm. "I wanted you to stop all this but they saw you with Ian and…"

"Ian is your brother Eamon. He needs us. He needs you. He has done nothing wrong."

Eamon pulled his hands away and dropped his eyes to the floor.

"If you don't go to the hearing on Wednesday they're going to disfellowship you for associating with apostates," he muttered returning to his chair sitting with his shoulders hunched, his back turned. "You're my wife and we're going there together."

"You're my husband. I'm not your child." Lyse tugged at his arm. "I won't be bullied and browbeaten with their phoney scriptures!"

Eamon shrugged. Defeated he shook his head. He writhed away from her tentative hand. He flinched at the touch of her fingers as they softly stroked the back of his neck. He edged away fixating on the dying fire with a tearing insight that caused his stomach to clench. He no longer knew how to share his life with this woman, his wife, without giving up his faith. And that was something he dare not do.

Chapter Eleven:
The Women's Room
Aileen

Joanie twisted the rusty latch then when nothing happened she put both hands onto the gate and pushed. Saorise and Niamh added their weight, small hands flat on the flaky wood, sturdy little legs splayed apart.

"Open sesame," they commanded, "Open sesame!"

Joanie rattled the latch again. "Open sesame," she yelled and pushed harder. "Open sesame!"

"Mammy!" Saorise called up to the open window, "Mammy we are all shuted out!"

Lyse managed to hop to the window, the plaster cast heavy and dragging. She pushed her blond head through the billowing net curtain.

"Sure it's only a bit stiff from the rain," she said grinning down at the upturned faces. "Give it a bit of a push."

"Here. Lookit." An unfamiliar deep voice came from behind Joanie and the girls. "Step aside."

A tall slender young woman tucked an unruly lock of red-black hair behind her ear and lifted a brown cowboy boot. "May I?" she asked Lyse with a sardonic grin.

Lyse looked at Joanie who shrugged and raised an eyebrow. "This is Aileen. We met her at the Spa and she's helped with the shopping."

"Go on then, give it a bit of a kick."

Aileen drew her foot back and with one swift hefty blow sent the door and the gate frame crashing into the garden.

Lyse a hand over her mouth stared down at the gaping hole in her back fence.

"Aileen plays for her works' women's five aside football team," Joanie said stepping over the debris, a child in each hand.

"I'd call that an own goal then." Lyse said beginning to laugh, "Eamon'll have a conniption fit. Come on in. The back door is already open...thankfully!"

"Well so," said Aileen as she and Joanie began to unpack the bags, "You didn't tell me your Lyse was such a looker."

"Shh." Joanie pushed the door to. "She's not *my* Lyse. She's an old married woman with a young one of her own. She knows nothing of bad girls like youes."

"She looks like a young one herself," said Aileen recalling the elfin face and the short mop of fair hair. "She can't be thirty yet. What's the husband like?"

"Eamon's a nice man." Joanie filled the kettle. "A bit weak and wet about his religion I suppose but," she turned to Aileen and added firmly, "she loves him right enough. So don't get any ideas and make trouble for her."

"I won't" Aileen promised her eyes round and innocent. "There's no harm in taking up a cup of tea and keeping her company while you get their dinner on."

***

Lyse

Lyse turned the book over in her hands. **The Women's Room. Marilyn French.** Was this another book Eamon would call apostate? She held it at arm's length and examined the quirky red and orange cover: **...*for every man who thought he knew a woman. For every woman who thought she knew herself.***

This friend of Joanie's, Aileen, had loaned her the book saying with a tone reverential
and solemn, "It's not just a novel but a book that changes lives."
Lyse smiled at the innocent irony of the remark. Her life had

changed far too drastically already. But still she may as well read it. She pushed it well under the bed deciding that like Eamon had with **Crisis of Conscience** it would be a secret read. Aileen had looked genuinely shocked when she had admitted to not having read a novel since her school days. She had said something like, "well, I'm truly sorry for that. A book like this should never be out of our hands. Knowledge is power." Lyse had wanted to explain about the Governing Body forbidding the reading of anything but their own literature but had politely, silently, accepted it instead.

She lay back suddenly tired and wiped another of the stray tears that seemed to leak unbidden these days. The plaster cast encased her right leg from toe to thigh. It was cold and clammy. Eamon had acted more cross than sympathetic when she had come home in a taxi after the accident. He had mostly moaned about the damage to the bicycle and then banged about in the kitchen leaving it in a mess. He had slept in his studio on the fold down bed leaving this morning with barely a "How are you" or a goodbye. His eyes cold, like they mostly were these days, his kiss also cold on her cheek.

Lyse sighed and turned her attention to the raucous laughter from the two girls who were down stairs having their tea. She sleepily speculated about Aileen. She dressed like a cowboy in checked shirt jeans and boots but was undeniably feminine. She had that lovely thick Irish hair, an enviable creamy freckled complexion. She had said her startling misty green eyes came from the tinkers in her family. She was a real talker too. The words tumbled from her like the soap bubbles Saorise loved to chase in the garden. She had described her work as an articled clerk and her prowess as an amateur jockey. She boasted she could ride almost any horse bare-backed. She asserted that one day a woman would win the Grand National; there would be a female Taoiseach; equal pay; contraception; divorce; abortion and any number of other outlandishly impossible things.

Lyse a smile playing about her lips pictured Ted Armstrong's face after having heard such talk and imagined that dark haired beauty riding bare-backed up the steps of the Kingdom Hall.

***

The Women's Centre

Lyse sat on the sagging sofa with her plastered leg plumped high with cushions. Every so often another woman would come over and ask to sign her cast until it was completely covered with scrawled names or a feminist symbol. Lyse lifted her leg and tried to decipher their meaning. "The clitoris is beautiful" was etched across the thigh length edge in a handsome cursive script. Aileen laughed as Lyse hastily covered it with the end of her blouse and said, "That's true right enough" and then wandered off into another room with a lanky untidy morose faced woman who had a stiff grey pigtail that reached way down her back.

Lyse fingered the carefully ironed creases in her first ever pair of jeans and was sorry she had not chosen a plainer top or borrowed a shirt from Joanie. Her makeup and blow dried hair felt oddly out of place in these shabby yet homely surroundings. None of these women dressed anything like her former witness friends or her neighbours. In **The Women's Room** Mira had hidden in the toilet but *her* leg had not held her prisoner. It was impossible to hop down the flight of stairs on her own to where she had seen **Wimmins** chalked over an original Ladies sign.

She picked up one of the paperback novels Aileen had thrown onto her lap trying not to glance across at two women happily squashed together in an armchair kissing. She forced her eyes onto the page and then squeezed them shut when biblical scenes of Sodom and Gomorrah, stern warnings from Leviticus and the words of St Paul began to imprint themselves on her brain. Yet there was something so compelling about their obvious passion for each other that almost made her envious.

Lyse was desperate for Aileen to come to the rescue. ***The Desert of the Heart*** failed to distract. She shoved the book and another with the disheartening title of ***The Well of Loneliness*** into her bag and rested her head on the sofa's arm. In the sudden silence of the emptying room she began to separate her jumbled impressions of Aileen's Women's Centre and the amorous couple.

Until today she had never doubted what love was. The Watchtower had schooled her in all kinds according to the ancient Greeks. Eros and Pragmia: meant exclusively for a husband; Philia: platonic love of friends; Agape: love of humanity; Storge for the family, especially your children but what about the kind of love she had just witnessed? Was that a love too…or the perversion the Bible and the organisation implied? Or was love just that …love?

Storge was straightforward. Saorise was her bright star: the love of her life. Eamon still held her heart but the chasm between them was now visible: her broken ankle a convenient excuse for him using the fold down bed in his studio. Even as they tidied the kitchen together there was a space between them at the sink as she washed and he dried. They had not made love for a long time or not what she thought of as making love. It was something sad and far more perfunctory than that. On the rare occasions he did come to her he was demanding and aloof, always carefully within the Watchtower's latest ever more intrusive bedroom rules. She could not remember the last time they had laughed inside or outside of the bedroom. His goodbye this morning, as always these days, had been chilly and remote.

She let the tears drop from her lashes and splash onto her cheeks stifling the urge to let out an anguished sob. She loved her husband but she hated those Witnesses who had driven such a wedge between them and…she almost despised him for letting them…for clinging onto something she knew he no longer completely believed in.

"Peg Leg!" Aileen said pulling a bare toe, "Wake up, time for your appointment at the hospital!"

Lyse's eyelids fluttered open in surprise. All those turbulent thoughts had somehow sent her to sleep. That was more than they did most nights. Perhaps this Women's Centre was as calming as Aileen insisted it was. It certainly made more sense than her life at home did these days.

Chapter Twelve:
Happy Birthday
Saorise and Eamon

Eamon stood for a moment watching his wife and daughter dancing around the kitchen. Saorise was a miniature replica of her mother. Their hair was the exact same shade of blond, their fair freckled skin and smile identical. Their hands and feet moved in unison. They were a pretty sight. Saorise was attempting the words of some new song. He went to the window and turned his ear to the glass but abruptly stepped back a frown wiping away his smile. His hand too heavy on the handle caused the door to swing open. Mother and daughter stared at him in surprise suspending their dance, the song dying on Saorise's lips.

Saorise glanced at each parent her lip quivering and quick tears brimming at the strange sight of Eamon's anger as he stood in the doorway his face pale his frown deepening. He stood for a long silent moment then marched to the table picking up a paper party bag and emptying its contents.

"What's this?" he examined an assortment of small sweets, a party hat, a balloon and a piece of iced cake, his face frozen, his voice low. "Where have these come from?"

"They be mine Da." Saorise began wiping at a tear with a small fist. "They's a party present from Grainne. She be four now. Mammy and me singed the birfday song."

The sight of Saorise's distress finally sank in. Eamon closed his mouth on an angry response his cheeks colouring into shame.

"Saorise love." said Lyse, slipping the gifts back into the bag. "Why don't you run upstairs and find your slippers. You can't be wearing your wellies at the tea table."

Saorise hesitated. "Are you cross Da?" she said her face creased with doubt, "they's only some sweets and things...you can have the cake if you like."

"No of course I'm not," Eamon said with an effort, "get your slippers like Mammy says or we'll never get our tea."

***

Eamon

Eamon continued to scrub the milk pan even after the small stain had gone. Then he turned his attention to clearing the table leaving the party bag untouched. Had Lyse left it there in silent recrimination? If she had it was working. He could hear them playing in the bathroom. Every so often Saorise's laugh wafted down through the ceiling. It was uncannily like the clear shrill sound of a flute; its sweet musicality was so completely hers. For a moment his stomach felt empty but the cause was not his only half eaten meal. It was the unspoken apology his little girl deserved. He reached for the bag deciding they could share its contents after a day or two but at the sound of Lyse's light step on the stairs he snatched his hand away.

"Shall I make us a cup of tea?" he said taking hold of the kettle and walking it to the tap.

"Alright so," Lyse said, "but first won't you go up and let Saorise know she has done nothing wrong?"

Eamon's face drained of colour as he thought of the scene through the window. His daughter had been crowing out the words of that song. Jehovah's Witnesses never teach their children it and Lyse knew that. Birthdays had never played a part in their family life, so why now? Guilt evaporated into the familiar tension that always seemed to flare between them these days.

"It's as if you deliberately look for ways to undermine me as...as... head of this household and I..." he trailed off recognising the kind of pomposity they had often cringed at together at meetings. He opened his mouth to rephrase, the words drying in his throat as he noticed the bible she held in her hand and the stickers between the pages.

"So am I not entitled to pick up one of these now Eamon?" Lyse said as if she could read his mind, "here then." She pushed the bible across the table and waited.

In the heavy silence that followed Eamon imagined he could feel the house shifting; hear an undisturbed floor board creak and his watch tick away at the remaining seconds of his marriage. He searched for his true wife in the face of this woman. He looked hard for his darling Margaret who had always supported him, had never thought to cross him but was confronted yet again by this incomprehensible lookalike. Exasperation and panic rose in his chest, his hand gripped the kettle, his mouth set into a stubborn line.

Lyse shrugged and sat down. She studied her husband with a similar uncomprehending stare. She picked up the party bag and took out a small wrapped sweet, slowly untwisting both ends of its cellophane wrapper.

"Remember the day our Saorise was born?" she said throwing him a ghost of her old smile. "Remember how we celebrated? The cards, the balloons, the cakes and the bottle of Guinness you gave me with a ribbon tide round the neck? You bought her first teddy bear."

"That was just the one time." Eamon faltered. "It's not what we..." he corrected himself, "alright what I do. It's not according to the Watchtower reading of the scriptures that says...well you know what they say...

"I know well what Ecclesiastes Seven says about the day of death being better," Lyse said, "but where does it say a birthday is against God's law?"

"The Watchtower is clear…it's clear…it clarifies…." Eamon knew his words lacked conviction, glimpsed a hint of mockery in her eyes. "I can't talk about these things with you anymore unless you…unless you…"

"What about Luke chapters one and two?" Lyse pressed, "Jesus had one great big birthday party didn't he? There were presents and shepherds, wise men and the like."

She dropped the sweet into her mouth. She held up the bag. "You aren't even convincing yourself," she said with the kind of teasing smile he could never resist. "Want one Mr. Hennessey?"

Eamon hesitated. His heart and hand itched to reach out. He was tired and he loved his wife. Perhaps he loved her and Saorise beyond all other things? He took a step forward and then another.

Lyse shook the bag "Yum yum," she grinned up at him smacking her lips.

At the sudden sound of a fierce rap and the sight of a shadowy figure framed against the window Lyse gave a startled yelp and dropped the bag. The contents tumbled and bounced off the table. Eamon, turning sharply immediately recognised the familiar shape of his brother.

"Is that Ian?" said Lyse, "Let him in. It's pishing down out there."

"I can't." Eamon shook his head, a shadow of distress travelled across his face. "He can't be here." He moved to the door and stood with his back to it. He fumbled with the key closing his fist over it.

Ian's knock came harder against the glass. "Eamon. Let me in."

"Don't be silly."Lyse hurried across. "He'll break the window."

"I just can't do this anymore." Eamon winced at the familiar voice pleading with him. He shook her hand away and opened his palm.

"Let him in then." Eamon said his face twisting as Lyse snatched at the key. He rushed from the room crushing sweets and cake underfoot as he went.

He stumbled up the stairs and into his art room. Without stopping to turn on the light he reached for the desk radio and dialled up the volume trying without success to drown out the awful sound of his brother still calling his name.

Chapter Thirteen:
The Good Samaritan
Ian

Maeve disappeared behind the swing doors. Ian, marooned and helpless squinted through the square of opaque glass. A shadow of a curtain pulled and a sudden anguished yell from inside had him hurrying away along the corridor. After a while he realised that the squeaky linoleum underfoot was betraying his alarm. He exchanged a rueful smile with the other fathers- to- be, sat down and tried to keep still.

At every footfall he lifted his head hoping against hope to see his older brother. He felt very young and very alone. It was impossible to shut out the cries of the women. The incessant piped music aggravated rather than calmed. He thought this must be the same tape, the same corridor and the self same doors he and Eamon had been trapped behind when Saorise was born. It had been a hard birth and had taken a long time. For a day and a half they had sat or stood or paced together. Once he had clung onto Eamon to keep him from pushing through those doors and later had taken him off to stop him shouting at the innocent midwife.

He swallowed down the bitter tepid leftovers of tea from the plastic cup. Where was *that* brother now it was his turn? Another pain laden cry filled the waiting room. Ian felt the urge to pray but realised with a sinking heart that he no longer knew how.

He searched his mind for reasons why he must have taken on so many of The Watchtower's nonsensical beliefs without question. Mam's stern Catholic ways had oppressed and then repelled him. Their father, now a vague memory, had been no more to him than a silent wraith sat under a blanket in the corner armchair. His only father figure was Eamon and Eamon's word was law and Eamon had been so certain.

"Ian...Ian lad. I've come to keep you company," said Lyse tugging at his sleeve. "Here I've made some sandwiches."

"Will she be alright?" Ian said relief flooding through him at the sight of his sister- in- law.

"Her waters broke a bit unexpected is all." Lyse unwrapped a sandwich and forced it into his hand. "Now eat this and stop worrying so."

"Why won't Eamon come? It's family it's..." Ian broke off and bit into the bread. "It's those elders isn't it?" He gave a helpless shrug. "They have him trapped somehow."

Lyse turned her attention to the flask and handed him a beaker of hot coffee. He silently ate through his pack of sandwiches and watched her pass round the extra to the other desperate men whose pale looks mirrored his own. His thoughts continually returned to Eamon who had stayed away, whose face had seemed so hard and alien when he had come to him looking for help. He wondered if his brother still realised what a lucky man he was to have Lyse and then with an uncomfortable presentiment doubted whether he was going to keep her unless he could break that iron grip of the Witnesses.

***

Eamon

Saorise finally drifted off mid-sentence still gabbling about her new cousin and asking after her mother. He sat for a while listening to her soft breath. He knew that all parents believe their children beautiful but still this little one, the child they had made from love, was a marvel to watch when sleeping. Again he noted how like her mother she was becoming with her golden curls; cherry coloured lips; long lashes that were turning from light to dark.

Recently she had begun to ask uncomfortable questions in a manner and tone uncannily like her mother's. She had asked whether he still loved Uncle Ian and in the same breath whether he had eaten Grainne's cake. She had, not incorrectly, tied the two topics together. Eamon fingered the razor cuts around his chin reflecting on Margaret Lyse's wry
comment that morning:

"Are you sure it's the blade?" she had said, "Perhaps your reflection worries you these days?"

She knew him so well and so, it seemed, did Saorise. He checked his watch. If only clocks really did stop and time turned back. If only he could decide what was the right path to take. If only he could be sure he could be a decent man without the organisation. If only he was certain that Jehovah would still exist in his heart without it. He could see the obvious cracks and flaws starting to appear in The Watchtower's increasingly strident articles. Thoughts of leaving meant the dreaded spectre of falling back into that old secret shameful life: a life not even his wife knew of, one she would never be able to understand.

Eamon reluctantly released the little fingers and crept down the stairs at the sound of footsteps outside. His stomach grew hollow at the sight of Ted Armstrong's shadow looming outside his front door. A niggling doubt suggested that fear was not what he was meant to feel when offered a shepherding call. But they had not offered had they? They had insisted and he had felt powerless to refuse. Margaret Lyse had not hesitated. She had waved those same unwelcome visitors away as if they were annoying buzzing little insects. He pictured the way she had turned her back and had walked from the Kingdom Hall as if it was the easiest thing in the world to do.

***

Lyse

Lyse was behind the driver's seat long before the bus reached her stop. She leapt from the platform when the bus had slowed. She began the uphill trudge at a jog, her heavy overnight bag clutched in both hands, pressed against her chest. The housing estate was only vaguely visible through the low fog that had fallen halfway through the journey from Ian and Maeve's. She imagined Saorise playing with Eamon in the bath or already listening sleepily to the Hungry Tiger and felt warmer. She quickened her pace up the endless incline and then through the labyrinth of roads leading to their block. She rounded the bend then slowed to a walk surprised to see the house in darkness.

Lyse hefted the bag awkwardly under an arm and searched her pocket for a key. Without the inside light and only the wan orange glow from a far off street light she struggled to find the lock. Using her fingers as a guide she finally managed to fit the key giving it an impatient twist. After two tries it still remained stiff and immovable. A sharp rap on the narrow glass did not prompt the kitchen light to spill into the hallway nor reveal Eamon's slight figure hurrying to her rescue. She pushed open the letter box calling his name then put an ear to the opening straining for a sound. There was only an empty silence.

Lyse leant back and looked up at the house. Every window was closed and every curtain drawn tightly shut without even the faintest glimmer of light behind. She upended her bag in a vain effort to find a back door key then stood for a moment blank faced and uncertain shaking her head compulsively as an unthinkable fear gradually took hold.

Carefully she retraced her steps to the corner wall and stumbled through the rubbish strewn waste ground that led to their back entrances. On Friday theirs was still just a gaping hole Eamon kept meaning to fix but now it was replaced by a thick wooden barrier. She recounted the gates in case she had somehow passed it in the fog. This was definitely the one. Even in the grey light she could see it was taller than the old gate. It was at least ten feet. She ran her hands up and down the heavy obstacle feeling for a latch but found just a dense piece of hardwood put in place to prevent entry.

"Think. Think." Lyse ordered herself, heart jerking, shocked tears making her eyes swim.
She thought to knock next door. She wondered if she could find her way downhill to the Maddens in this fog. Was Eamon asleep in the

chair beside Saorise's bed? Was there any point in calling out? Would she be yelling into an empty space? "Think. Think." A slow thought began to push through her panic. Lyse rubbed a sleeve across her eyes, squinting through the thick yellowish smog mixed with chimney smoke. A few paces to her right the brick shapes she had tripped over on the way round were just visible.

Each one she lifted cut at her hands and bruised her wrists but she persisted placing them together two by two until she had built a sizeable step. She stacked the final three one on top of the other. Oblivious to the stinging grazes or the precarious ascent she clambered up grabbing at the top of the wall. Her chest heaving with effort she swung her legs over the edge and then leapt into what she hoped was the shadow of the soft sandpit below.

***

Lyse woke with a start in the cold light of a grey morning. For a merciful second all seemed as it should be until the strange quiet, the discomfort of the narrow cot bed sliced through her half dreaming mind. The creeping horror of the night before jerked her fully awake as she looked around the room in renewed disbelief. Saorise's wardrobe door hung open, the inside empty of her winter clothes. Toys, books, the teddy she would never be without were all gone. Even her paper lantern from play school was missing.

With each step she added to the inventory of Saorise's missing things: her best coat, her favourite wellington boots and her miniature umbrella. A single small sock lay on the bottom stair. A set of Eamon's paints was upended and scattered half way along the hall. At the kitchen door Lyse paused her heart thumping as she steeled herself for the sight of broken glass and the memory of the hammer blows smashing at the window until it had splintered and finally gave way.

Lyse searched again for the note she had somehow hoped to find the night before. She carefully walked the room checking every drawer and shelf until she reached the sink stacked with their best china. Three cups, three saucers, the tea tray, a plate for biscuits, silver tea spoons...who had Eamon taken these down for? She reached in and selected a cup as if its dregs might hold the answer. A meaty hand spooning in sugar came first to mind, then the owner's imposing presence crystallised into a name. As if *that* hand had squeezed her throat she gasped gripping the handle until it snapped. She wrenched the basin from the sink and with one swift movement threw it to the far corners of the room, chasing the falling crockery and stamping it into the floor, yelling words she had no idea she had known, cursing her husband, the god and his agents who had taken her child.

***

A frantic knocking finally penetrated the wretched numbness that had quickly followed on from her fading rage. Her eyes, swollen and stinging were slow to open at the sound of the familiar voice that repeatedly called her name. Lyse was surprised to find herself on the floor. Carefully she picked her way through the wreckage of her prized possessions and the lethal shards of glass unsure whether she had somehow fallen into a fitful sleep or had simply fainted from exhaustion.

Fazed by the impossibility of opening the door, Lyse stood helpless and shaking until Joanie yelled at her through the letter box:

"Hurry the feck up and open a window in the living room!"

There was a moment of panic as she moved with leaden feet to the windows. Eamon had not thought to use the window locks as she had feared. After a hard push the window stiffly opened and Joanie clambered through her face emerging through the curtains, pink with effort and concern.

"What the feck is going on here?" Joanie said taking hold of the swaying Lyse whose relief at her rescue had brought on another choking bout of tears. "What the feck?" Joanie repeated "What the feck?"

Lyse was sat on a stool and obediently lifted her face to be wiped and her cuts to be cleaned. With a dim relief she realised she was being taken care of in the way Joanie did with her unruly younger brothers and sisters. She drank the steaming tea heavily laced with sugar without protest and eventually managed to give a halting account of last nights' discovery.
"What am I going to do Joanie?" she said, fresh tears beginning to slip beneath painful lids. "What? I don't know what to do."

"I'll tell you what," said Joanie wringing the tepid flannel and once again wiping it roughly over her face, "We're going to get Rory up here to change those locks and to fix the window. Then we're going to find that feckin' husband of yours and I'm going to kick him to death."

Lyse had never seen Joanie look so angry. Her bright eyes had darkened into points of black fury, her usual white toothed smile absent. Lyse realised her friend was in deadly earnest and despite everything she felt a laugh rising in her throat as she replied:

"Then you'll have to get in front of me. I'm having first kick."

Joanie grinned, "That's the spirit. Now you go up and get out of those manky things. I'll freshen up the bed for you to have a sleep."

"I can't" Lyse shook her head, "I can't sleep when I don't know where she is."

"You can." said Joanie taking a small box from her pocket and shaking a small round pill into her palm, "You'll sleep right enough with one of these. Don't look like that they're one of me Mammy's, she swears by them."

***

New glass glinted above the back door, a reassuring key protruded from a sturdy metal lock. The wreckage of china was tided away, the washed floor shone wetly in the weak afternoon sun. Lyse felt her heart lift a little as Joanie put a match under the kettle.

"Rory's gone to get doors," she said, "and lookit.." she pointed through the new window to where the fearsome barrier lay propped against the wall, "when you're ready we can go out from there on our bikes and find some help."

"Help?" Hope dropped away as she contemplated whom Eamon may have gone to with Saorise. "There's not a witness in the world that will help me," she said flatly and sat down ready to cry.

"Stop that!" Joanie commanded shoving the mug into her hands, "Sure enough *they* won't but I've been thinking about those *ex* ones that will."

"Ian won't know. I don't want to tell him what his brother has done." Lyse imagined Ian's face if she were to tell him. He would be mortified. He would be angry.

"Not him," Joanie said with triumph as if she were about to pull a rabbit from a hat, "but those two old ones you told me about, with the children that won't talk to them."

Lyse put the mug down, "Leo and June!" she stood up, "Yes they only live this side of Tallaght.

"Sit yourself down and eat this sandwich first," Joanie said, "I can't have youes fainting on the road and..." she paused to produce another rabbit, "I've got an idea how Aileen can put the frighteners on them that's behind all this because you can bet it's not just your stupid eejit of a husband."

***

June

June hesitated at the top of the stairs trying to identify the two figures through the picture glass of their front door. A ring from the bell always arrived unexpected these days. First, she experienced the usual dull disappointment. It was not Martha or Simon there were no welcome sounds of her grandchildren clamouring and calling "Mamo, Mamo". It would not be her oldest friends Lynette or Roisin or any of the myriad of brothers and sisters from their former spiritual family. June took off her reading glasses and studied the two outlines, one tall the other a good few inches shorter but recognisable as Margaret Lyse.

Leo was in the garden. Even in this weather he had to keep busy. He dug his garden. She knitted too many jumpers and cardigans for just the two of them. The bell rang again and this time she hurried to open the door putting a smile on her face and her disappointments behind her.

The two followed her into the kitchen. June sat them down masking her shock at Margaret Lyse's drawn face and swollen eyelids. She smiled at her young companion, liking the look of her dark helmet of glossy hair; wide open smile and offered them tea.

June listened quietly her eyes growing troubled and wet as Lyse brokenly began her tale. As she faltered Joanie took over her voice shaking indignantly and using the type of language that had June wincing relieved that Leo had not yet noticed their visitors and come in.

"It doesn't help I know," June said when Joanie had finally run out of steam, "but I've read of this happening a few times in America and in Britain but never here." A germ of an idea then presented itself. "I need to call in Leo. The one thing I do know is that there is too much local scandal for them already. Arnold Massey at the Branch Office won't want another one. If you're brave enough my dear let's see if Leo will call someone he's just got to know from the Irish Times."

"Oh she's brave enough." Joanie ignored her friend's horrified glance grabbing her hand under the table and giving it a hard squeeze, "and they can have some pictures I took before Rory got to mending things."

A burning hatred and a thirst for revenge ran through Lyse sweeping away the helpless weakness that had afflicted her only moments before. "Do you think they'll be interested?" she asked suddenly doubtful.

June nodded, "I think they just might," she said cautiously with a belated thought that perhaps she should have checked with Leo before raising their hopes.
"You bet they will!" Joanie said beaming, "this is Catholic Ireland remember. They hates Jova's and anyone else that don't go along with their ways of believing."

"They've got that in common with the Witnesses then," said June with an irony knew to Lyse. She opened the kitchen door and beckoned to Leo. This Joanie was a breath of fresh air. She reminded her a little of Martha's oldest, an irrepressible imp but she was just what was needed at a time like this.

***

The following afternoon Joanie persuaded Lyse out of her tracksuit and ransacked her meagre wardrobe in search of something suitable.

"You don't have a lot do you?" Joanie said not striving for tact, "all those frumpy ole Jova clothes. When this is over we've shopping to do."

This morning's visit to the local Garda to register Saorise as missing had been awful. She had cried her way all though her statement which could not help but condemn Eamon as a criminal. She had left there feeling soiled and humiliated; almost angry with Aileen and Joanie who had insisted it was necessary. She had barely been able to thank Aileen for arranging a free appointment with her boss at Dardis and Dunns.

Lyse dutifully changed into the sensible skirt and dark jumper and tried to steady her roiling nerves as they waited for the journalist and camera man to arrive. In between waves of energising thoughts of hope and revenge her mood would droop. Saorise's photograph lay on the bed ready. She blanched at the thought of that little face plastered all over the front pages of a newspaper. How had she and Eamon come to this? Was there nothing left of her once happy marriage and Saorise's carefree childhood?

At the sound of a car drawing into their driveway Lyse shook herself free of fruitless regrets. None of that mattered for now. She would bring Saorise home whatever it might cost and however she might have to pay for it in the future.

Chapter Fourteen:
Let your Will be done
Roisin and Jimmy
(Five days later).

Eamon was pacing the short length of their balcony again. Jimmy crossed to the window and pulled the curtains but the restless shadow was still visible through the thin cotton. He sighed and sat on the bed pulling off his shoes and socks.

"How long Jimmy?" Roisin asked, "We can't manage like this for long. The place is far too small."

"Shh…" Jimmy hissed, "Eamon'll hear you."

Roisin lowered her voice. "The boys don't want to share with a little girl."

Jimmy shook his head and shrugged. "As long as Eamon and the elders want us too, I suppose."

Roisin continued to wrestle with her thick curly hair all the while fighting the desire to say what was on her mind. Eventually she lay down the brush and turned to her husband, noting his frown; a sure sign he was not willing to be challenged too far.

"I know it's your decision Jimmy," she said, "but are you certain it's not a crime what we've done?"

"Eamon is her father. He has the right to take Saorise away from anything he thinks is corrupting her spiritual well- being." His look was sharp. "People leave and do all kinds of things you wouldn't expect."

Roisin stared at him swallowing down a surprised retort. It was uncomfortable to hear Brother Armstrong's tone coming from her usually reasonable husband.

"Jimmy. I know Margaret Lyse has left the truth," she said carefully, "but I can't imagine for one minute she would be doing anything that could be called corrupting can you?" She waited and when he refused to comment she pressed. "At least go to him and ask what's going on. Make sure it's what he wants and not what..." she hesitated loath to openly criticise the elders, "...well just ask him won't you?"

Jimmy looked at his wife and then at Eamon's dejected figure still outside, still endlessly pacing the few short steps before turning and pacing; turning and pacing. He reached under the bed for his shoes.

"Alright so," he said reluctantly, "I'll ask him but if I can't tell you what he says you mustn't ask me. And if we have to keep them here we will."

Roisin nodded, "Of course if it's Jehovah's will then of course." She waited until she saw Jimmy join Eamon on the balcony before switching off the light and beginning her prayers:

"Dear Jehovah God can it ever be right to steal a child away from her mother?" she whispered. "Let your will be done... not theirs."

***

Eamon

Eamon shook his head when Jimmy suggested they should go back inside. He leaned over the rail and stared vacantly across the sprawling Dublin landscape lit by a thousand homes and the sparse road lights of the Naas Road snaking through the city. Their conversation had only increased his doubts. Jimmy had listened respectfully but even as he had listed his reasons he knew they sounded too thin: his actions extreme and incomprehensible. He had not dared to repeat the gossip about some of Margaret Lyse's new friends, or where in Dublin she had been seen with them. His Margaret Lyse would never take Saorise into such a world. Why had he so willingly believed everything the elders had insinuated?

He shivered in the biting November cold as he finally let the heat of blinding insight in: his own guilt and self doubts had kept him a prisoner to a poisonous organisation that did untold damage to everyone it touched. He had clung to that false faith and turned from his wife. He had repaid all her trust and love and loyalty by shutting her out of his heart and then her own house. He had run away with the one she loved the most because of his ridiculous jealousy. He had implicated others by his actions. He had gone further than even the elders must have anticipated. The consequences were too appalling to contemplate. His hands gripped at the rail, his knees shook as he fought the terrible urge to simply throw himself down the six flights onto the concrete play park below.

"Eamon! Eamon! Come on in now why don't you?" Jimmy's hand gripped his arm, pulling him through the open door. "Lookit...you're scaring Saorise she's crying for her Mammy."

Eamon stood dazed and momentarily uncomprehending. His heart pumped erratically. His breath came in ragged shocked gasps. Each man stared horrified at the other. What had he so nearly done? It was already unthinkable. When Roisin came to the door with Saorise Jimmy waved them away and knelt in front of his friend keeping a firm grip on his arm, beginning a murmured prayer.

"I need to get home." Eamon cut in his voice rising. "I need to go home and make things right." He shook off Jimmy's hand and started towards the bedroom. "I need to get Saorise and take her back."

"It's the middle of the night." Jimmy walked Eamon back to his chair. "I'll go with you as far as the Post Office in the morning. You could use the telephone and call Brother Armstrong first. He could bring his car and help with your bags."

Eamon shook his head, his whole being recoiling at the thought. "No. That's the last thing I should do!" The vehemence of his words took them both by surprise. Jimmy stiffened. A puzzled caution clouded his face. Eamon sensed a chilly irretrievable distance grow between them.

"I'll make us a cup of tea then." said Jimmy. "Then we should get some sleep."

Eamon watched his friend's retreating back with a sharp pang of contrition. As loyal brothers and sisters Jimmy and Roisin had willingly given him their support. With a sinking heart he realised that they too could expect only suspicion and censure from these elders. The entire organisation was mired in a quicksand of paranoia.

As Eamon quietly sipped his tea he realised that this night when he had stood on the brink of the unknown he had finally understood why Margaret Lyse had wanted to set them free. And why she had walked away from the Kingdom Hall with such a light heart and with the words:

"Whatever God is, it's not this."

***

Jimmy

At first light Jimmy gave up trying to find sleep. His mind continually returned to the sight of Eamon. He remembered with a shudder the blank expression and the way one leg was raised high on the rail, as if he might jump. Had he wanted to...would he have...? Traffic noise and thin sunshine filtered through the thin curtains. The alarm clock clicked to seven. By twenty past he was already dressed and stealthily crossing the living room where Eamon lay sleeping, facing the wall, his back tightly curled.

He paused only for a glass of water before leaving the flat and taking the shabby lift down the six flights. He hurried towards the Post Office checking his pockets for change, resolving to call Brother Armstrong despite Eamon's objections. He contemplated other names: someone less strident, perhaps Brother Berri or Flowers. Ted would not take too kindly to that. He was a proud man, a little too proud maybe but unswerving in his desire to keep their congregation clean and together.

Jimmy continued on his way with a slower step, heart sore and perplexed as he thought of those who had inexplicably fallen away this past year. They had all seemed such strong and sound spiritual men and women. Leo and June Johnson had been the first to bring him and Roisin into the truth. Leo had been the elder who had married them and June the one who had supported Roisin through the difficulties of pregnancy and childbirth. He knew Roisin missed June's friendship deeply just as he felt the loss of Leo's wise counsel. And now his best friend Eamon had lost his wife to the scourge of apostasy and appeared to be in danger of losing *his* way entirely. At that thought Jim quickened his pace as the sandstone bullet scarred columns of Parnell Street Post Office came into view. He must put his faith in Jehovah's true servant and telephone Brother Armstrong.

***

Jimmy backed out of the cubicle, ears still ringing with the peremptory demand from his brother elder to put the telephone down and buy The Irish Times. His finger ends searched his trouser pocket linings as he darted across the road towards the newspaper stand outside Dunnes. He threw all the spare coins, uncounted, into the box and strode away, not stopping until he reached the quiet park in Stephen's Green.

He read the front page by-line still standing, his mouth dropping open as Saorise's four year old face smiled innocently back at him. The stark words: **Kidnapped by Jehovah's Witnesses** struck him like a blow between the eyes.

Jimmy found an empty bench and opened the centre pages to the main article. A fresh assault of photographs lay in wait: a tear stained Margaret Lyse, a broken window and a huge barrier fixed between the breeze blocks of a back entrance He read the text hurriedly and then carefully. Surely he had only done as Eamon and the elders had asked? Hadn't Ted told him he must do his Christian duty: Jehovah's Will? Hadn't he acted in good faith to protect a young girl in spiritual danger? This morning though, Ted with a voice shaking with righteous indignation had seemed to imply that this was all down to him and Eamon. A solicitor's letter representing a Mrs Hennessey had already arrived at the Dublin Branch and was in the hands of the Overseer. His parting shot had been a stern warning that their actions had brought the organisation into disrepute and that there would be consequences.

His eyes wandered across the green where a small boy crowed with delight as he and his mother threw breadcrumbs to the ducks that had gathered in a quacking whirling mass at the pond side. His smile faded as he realised his own simple godly life had suddenly grown complicated and dangerous. The paper had called it kidnapping. The Garda might come to their home and arrest him. Would anyone see his actions as those prompted by the desire to do God's Will? Was

Brother Armstrong's behaviour this morning that of a loving shepherd?

Jimmy at last accepted that he could not put his news off any longer and hurried home. The boys were at school. Saorise's little red coat and Eamon's rough donkey jacket had gone from the coat rack. The sofa bed was neatly folded away. He flattened the paper he had been clutching in a tight fist, pushing it down into his jacket pocket.

His relief to find their guests missing was tempered by the thought of facing Roisin. She had only done as a good Christian wife should. She had taken Eamon and Saorise in without voicing any opposition or reservations. This was going to mean trouble not just for him but for her too. He debated whether as head of the household he could begin with an apology or at least an admission that her unspoken fears had proven true. He pulled a chair to the table and shrugged off his jacket, careful to fold the bulky pocket inwards and out of sight.

Roisin with the briefest of smiles passed him the breakfast she had put aside and poured him a cup of tea before quietly going about her unfinished chores. He ate slowly, chewing and swallowing noisily to fill the silence whilst the paper sat uneasy in his pocket, its headlines branding Eamon and the organisation as kidnappers and he, or possibly they, albeit as yet unnamed, accomplices.

Roisin took away his empty plate. She poured them both more tea and sat opposite, patiently waiting until he could bring himself to lift his head and look at her. As he reached for his jacket she took a copy of the Irish Times from her lap and pushed it across the table, searching his face for answers.

"What have we done Jimmy?" she said, "Did we do wrong?"

"We... no *I* did what I thought was Jehovah's Will but now ..." Jimmy lapsed into silence. He studied the awful condemnatory words writ large in black ink as he struggled for the answer: what *had* he done? What *had* they all done? Whose will *had* been done?

Chapter Fifteen:
Finding Lyse
Joanie

"Bejasus the cheek of the man!" Joanie muttered as she carried on sweeping the slivers of planed wood until Saorise began to run the final few steps up to the house.

"Joanie! Joanie I's back from my venture."

Joanie resisted the urge to pick the child up and run her into the house. She plastered a smile on her face instead.

"Quick!" she said, "You go in. Your Mammy and Niamh can't wait to see you."

She gave the pile of splinters another brisk push down the drive before lifting the broom head level with Eamon's chest. "You jackeen...you...you gurria you... you...!"

Eamon backed away, dropping Saorise's bag of toys, suddenly aware there was an audience on every doorstep.

"Can you just let me into my own house Joanie?" Eamon said with an effort, a weak smile of embarrassment on his lips. His pale complexion coloured at the beginnings of catcalls behind him.

Joanie lifted the broom as high as his face taking a step forward. "Don't you move you weak willed slob you, you excuse for a man, you..."

"It's ok Joanie you can put that down. He's not coming in" said Lyse calmly from the doorway. "It's my name on the Corporation papers

Eamon." She threw him a cold look, "You must have forgotten. This is my house not yours."

Rory joined Lyse, a spanner hanging loosely from a huge fist, "Shall I give your man a crack with this?"

Joanie slowly lowered the broom, grinning as Gerry Fagin called across, "Go on let the Jova gombeen have it!"

"Margaret love just let me in for a talk is all." Eamon pleaded just managing to stand his ground. "For the love of God let me in."

"And whatever kind of god might that be?"Joanie scoffed raising the broom again. "Not *your* kind that's a sure thing."

Lyse swiftly intervened persuading the makeshift weapon away from Joanie, "Go on inside. I can do this," she said, "I can do this by myself."

Joanie reluctantly retreated towards the house with her brother. She paused and threw Eamon a final ferocious glance. "Alright so but I swear I'll swing for ya if I get the chance. You eejit!"

***

Lyse

Lyse picked up the fallen toys and walked them back to the hall then wordlessly sorted through each bag until she had collected everything that was Saorise's. The remainder she left where they lay on the grass verge. She went across to the small garden wall and sat arms folded with her back to their neighbours, waiting until they went inside.

Eamon, his face flaming sat down. He flinched as she moved away rubbing his thinning hair distractedly pushing it back and forth. The gesture was so poignant and familiar it almost weakened her resolve. Deliberately she relived each moment of the past five days:

the shock of finding her home barricaded; the fearful climb in the fog and the frantic hammer blows against glass; the wardrobe open and empty; the terrifying long nights and days that had followed: the awfulness of their private life laid bare to the press, the police and the law.

Lyse turned to face her husband aware that he must have begun speaking a while ago. She stared at his desperate face, at his writhing mouth making muddled apologetic explanations that made no sense. She moved a fraction further away each time a sentence held the words "degraded worldly life" or "Jehovah" or "the truth" or "the elders" until the wall ended forcing her to stand.

"Eamon stop!" she said impatient to be away. "You best go to your mother's or back to where you came from or Ted Armstrong's if he'll have you," she concluded turning towards the house, "oh and take your things with you. I'll pack the rest tomorrow."

"Wait!" Eamon hurried to reach her before the door closed. "Wait. Please think about us, our marriage. Saorise. Margaret I love you. I love Saorise, you know that don't you?"

Lyse, her eyes turning inward and distant, looked at the man she had promised to love and cherish and found a stranger in his place. She thought back to the day when their life had begun to unravel, the exact moment when Margaret had irretrievably lost her faith but had begun to find Lyse. She remembered leaning into that warm whitewashed wall with her face up to the welcome sun. Eamon had not followed her. He knew even then, why she had to leave and why he should too but he had chosen that life, kept his name and clung to his false god.

"I'm Lyse, Eamon," she said with a finality he was never to forget. "Margaret is in the past along with whatever your god and your love is supposed to mean."

Lyse closed the door. She clicked the latch and drew the bolt behind her beginning her second walk towards freedom and a future where, perhaps, anything was going to be possible...for her and for Saorise.

Epilogue:
"Find your freedom wherever you find your truth" c.s.2020

Lyse
1988

Lyse watched as Saorise hopped, skipped and jumped across the playground, her bright red "grown-up" satchel bouncing on her back. She and her new best friend Cerys had already embarked on one of those spontaneous and intense little girl conversations. Their two heads, one blond the other dark, were almost touching as they disappeared through the entrance without a backwards glance or a final wave goodbye. Lyse had a poignant memory of the four year old Saorise doing much the same thing with Niamh when she had joined the Water-Babies. Then she had been proud and relieved at her daughter's confidence and now she marvelled at her ten year old resilience in the face of so much change. Lyse lingered as she had at the poolside five years earlier, just to be sure, before turning away to find her bus stop.

Lyse waited impatiently, her eyes scanning the road ahead, willing the bus to materialise way before its due time. Her interview was in forty five minutes. She wished she had thought to ask Jill or Betty to give her a few tips or that she had at least read the university prospectus in full. She wondered now why she had done neither of those eminently sensible things. The very idea that she might actually be offered a place still seemed an impossibility of epic proportions. She had hardly dared do more than complete the complicated application form. She had only done that because of the continual prompting of her friends and night school tutor, Mrs Stokes.

As she boarded the bus and climbed the stairs for a better view of the passing streets she contemplated the hilly terrain and car strewn roads with a growing unease. Cardiff was a far cry from the empty lane ways and short cuts of Clondalkin. She should get a better bike with gears and lights. A helmet was a definite and maybe one of those yellow rain jackets. She sighed. It would all cost money but cheaper in the long run than the bus. Being what was euphemistically called a single parent had its downside but the alternative, well that was out of the question.

The latest letter from Eamon was still unopened in her bag and had sat there like a ticking bomb since Tuesday. Two other envelopes had arrived this morning. The smart Basildon Bond blue was obviously from June. The bulky reused brown one with Hennesey Motors crossed out, was from Ian or more precisely from Maeve, little Margaret and baby Thomas.

Lyse took out the one from June which began as the familiar careful cheery newsletter that made no mention of their still estranged children and grand children. The first page was all about the summer garden, her new greenhouse and the gardening club she had finally joined. Lyse smiled at the phrase "they've voted for me to organise the Show. I don't know why but well, since they've asked..." June was such a practical and capable woman. At long last she was allowed to let her own light shine rather than modestly hide it under the proverbial bushel.

She turned the page surprised not to find the usual cutting from Leo's latest column from the Irish Times pinned to the corner. June always proudly included that and whatever finding he had unearthed in his seemingly never ending research into the false doctrines from The Watchtower's publications. She turned the paper to the window. The writing always a little shaky had slipped a little and the ink indentation was lighter on this page. Each sentence was more stilted than the one before. Quick tears sprang to her eyes and fell onto the letter smudging the words recounting Leo's stay in hospital; the stroke that had left him without the use of his right arm; his difficulties with speech and June's brave hopeful words that perhaps Martha and Simon may now decide to visit.

The bus jerked to a stop at a red light. Lyse glanced at her watch and tried to turn her attention to her interview. The untidy road on the right was a long line of boarded-up shop fronts, and a used car showroom with a petrol station. At the end, in stark contrast with all else, there stood a neat low red bricked building. Lyse rubbed at the steamy glass with her sleeve taking a closer look. There it was: the familiar neat white lettering above the doorway: **Kingdom Hall of Jehovah's Witnesses**.

Lyse slowly folded June's letter away and put Ian and Maeve's aside for another time. She stared through the mud splattered window at the disappearing building and took a last look at the message below the sign: **Open to the public. All are welcome.** The breathtaking irony of that statement pierced at her heart as she thought grimly of the wickedness of a religion that deliberately separated parents from children; wives from husbands.

Deep into her past Lyse more or less slept walked off the bus and along Windsor Place. She had still not given any thought to her impending interview. And now she was at the imposing door. She hesitated fighting a pressing urge to simply turn away. If she stepped through; gave her name to the smart looking woman behind the glass counter there would be no turning back.

Lyse sat in the quiet ante-room waiting for her name to be called, staring up at the stucco ceilings; down at the squares of marble flooring and then across at the serious dark paintings on the oak panelled walls. This was more than just a building. It was a temple: a temple whose only god was education.

Her name was called. It was time. She boldly pushed her way through the swing doors towards her future. A shadowy picture of Margaret, not quite Lyse, going through another set of similar doors swiftly flitted through her mind's eye. As she shook hands with the tall elegant bearded man and the strangely dressed woman in a yellow pant suit her thoughts at last became clear and sharply focussed. This temple was hers to worship in if she wanted it. It could be her freedom: her truth.

Later as she retraced her steps with their provisional offer ringing repeatedly in her ears Lyse began to think of her life as almost mended: a jigsaw with all its colours and shapes finally piecing themselves back together. Anything *was* possible and *nothing* out of the question.

Eamon
1988

Eamon drew his eye across his well stacked paper shelf, selecting and then almost immediately, rejecting his choice. This letter was the most important of his life. If the paper was wrong it would be impossible to write. And it had to be written and it had to be today. Eventually he opted for an A4 white wove deciding to rule the lines with one of his wooden dip pens and then use the Parker Sonnet that Margaret had given him as a wedding gift.

He quickly became engrossed and calmed by the meticulous detail of ruling his exact straight lines. It was a strategy he had used since a boy, a reason to stay away from the oppressive downstairs until his mother tired of her prayers or her repetitive monologues directed at his near silent Da. An hour passed before he was finished and remembered, with a sinking heart, the task ahead.

So he went to his inks drawer and spent a further fifteen minutes examining each small glass bottle in turn. Should he use the remainder of his Montblanc black or the J Herbin Celebration blue? He picked up the Montblanc with the ghost of an amused grin. Writing to ask his wife for a divorce was hardly a cause for celebration.

Eamon stared down at the page, blank save the word **Dear** hesitating for a long moment. **"Margaret"** was on the tip of his tongue. His nib itched to inscribe the letter **M**. He and his pen, it seemed, still resisted that other name. He struggled to stay in his seat. He had to write the name **Lyse**. He had to write the word divorce and he had to write them today.

For a while he let his mind drift to all those letters he had written to "his Margaret" before and after they had married. He pictured the bright colours he had used, the extravagant hearts and flowers he had painted on cards, always with the letter **M** using his calligraphy to its best advantage. He remembered the time and care he had taken over their five anniversaries; her favourite was the jigsaw he had taken months to make or maybe the toy town bus with **Number One** on the front and **My Margaret** after **Destination**?

He delayed a further five minutes speculating whether he dare suggest that this time he could bring Saorise home with him for the holidays. He wished that by now she could trust him but knew deep down why not and why her being granted sole custody had been right and just. At least she had never stopped him visiting. He picked up the pen: *Lyse*. He wrote each sentence slowly and with artistic precision. He was careful not to let his heart show through the words. He wrote exactly as he had been told he should and not a word more.

Eamon had to chase the postman's van as it was leaving the curb. He stuck his hand through the open window waving the letter and begging for it to be taken in. He was glad it was Mrs Mahoney's son or he would have been out of time and out of luck. He watched the van receding into the distance, calling his thanks, waiting until it was out of sight.

"Goodbye my Margaret," he said, shoving his hands in his pockets, blinking away the very last of his tears and decided to take the long walk to the meeting rather than wait for the bus.
At first, he walked with his head down hurrying through the housing estate hoping not to run into one or other of the Madden's. He skirted the tennis courts and the pool experiencing the usual bitter-sharp twist of resentment. If White's Farm had never been built over they would not exist and his marriage may not have ended. He shrugged away that thought as ridiculous. It had been *his* doubts, *his* indecision, *his* groundless jealousy, *his* rash over reaction of taking Saorise away.

The stroll in the warm July evening air and the prospect of being able to tell the brother elders that he had posted the letter eventually cheered him. He quickened his pace taking the shortcut through the lane and hurried towards the Kingdom Hall whose familiar red bricks and solid compact shape suddenly felt as it had used to: safe and as reassuring as his own home once was.

He wondered how soon he would be reinstated after his divorce was finalised. Ted had assured him that it would be recognised by the congregation. He allowed himself to imagine the day when he would no longer have to slink through the side entrance and stand at the back. He looked forward to staying for the final prayer when his former brothers and sisters would not be obliged to shun him. He would be welcome to linger. To worship with them. Remake old friendships and forge new ones.

Perhaps one day Catholic Ireland would allow divorce. Maybe he would be free to find a wife who wanted the same truths that he did. His thoughts briefly turned to the quiet and gentle Mary Flowers. Surely it was a possibility? Not quite out of the question... was it?

The End

Printed in Great Britain
by Amazon

81565161R00058